JOHN DEJANOVICH

Who's Next...?
by John Dejanovich

ISBN: 9781728775661

First print edition: October 2018
First electronic edition: October 2018, Version 1.0

Cover Photo: The cover photo is a digitally recreated version of the famous P-38 fighter named "Yippee", taken over Burbank, California. It is intended as a tribute to the Lockheed Corporation's magnificent contribution to the war effort and to Lt. Floyd Fulkerson is the only pilot to fly it on a combat mission.

Contents

To all the fighter pilots in the US Army Air Force who served in the SWPA during World War II

Prologue

In the end, with the passage of time, the how's and why's and who caused this and that matter only in the context of ongoing global history. For the players...the everyday struggles of everyday people, it is and was about serving and perfecting their combat skills, in order to give themselves the best opportunities and choices about surviving.

This then is the story of ordinary men who would ride the charge of events to levels of extraordinary performance and emotion. It is fair and safe to say that they possessed skills conducive to their roles and probably beyond the abilities of most fellow warriors.

They represent two radically different cultures and within their own specific countries they were separated by equally huge class gulfs. However, they came to their missions on an equal playing field.

Join me now, in a look back at the drama that was the air war in the SWPA between the Sky Warriors of Japan and the fighter drivers of the US Army Air Force.

This book is dedicated to all the men who served in that effort But, especially to the following:

Major Richard I. Bong:

- Buried Poplar, Wis.
- "Ace of Aces"
- 40 Combat Kills
- Died in air crash 6 Aug 45 testing P-80 jet fighter Burbank, Cali.

Major Thomas B. McGuire Jr.:

- 38 Combat kills
- Buried Arlington National Cemetery
- KIA 7 Jan 45 Negros Is Philippines

1LT Floyd L. Fulkerson

- Silver Star
- Distinguished Flying Cross
- Bronze Star
- Purple Heart
- Died 30 Oct 2017, Little Rock, Ark.

Saburo Sakai:

- IJN Fighter Pilot
- Survived WWII Lived normal life
- 63 Combat Kills

Nishina Nakajima:

- IJN Fighter Pilot
- KIA Philippines 1945
- 84 Combat Kills

Who's Next...?

The Awakening

We were staying with my mom's sister for the summer. Something about getting me out of the big city for a while...for my own good, whatever that meant. I was 15 when this started and it was late spring in Poplar. Early June to be exact and with the icy grip of winter finally past the leaves had unfurled, the new grass was brilliant but, still short and everywhere buds and flowers were popping open. I was out riding my bike and for no particular reason I had followed the narrow paved lane out of town and ultimately rode into the local cemetery near Poplar Creek. Why, I do not recall, maybe I thought I would park my bike there and visit the nearby creek to see how it was flowing. As it turned out I never got to the creek.

I remember seeing this older gentleman on the far West side of the cemetery He was studying a plot beneath a large oak. As I circled through the paved pathway he turned and walked toward his car in the parking lot and soon he entered it and drove away. I had never seen him before and out of adolescent curiosity I walked over to the graves beneath the tree. There were several generations of the same name buried here. It looked like all the way back to the grandparents.

As I studied the gravestones one in particular stood out. It was a simple flat stone slab of normal size. It read as follows:

Richard Ira Bong
Major Fifth Air Force
Sept. 24, 1920–Aug. 6, 1945
"America's Ace of Aces"

Beneath it separated by about an inch of grass another more decorative marble stone. This one was inlaid with gold lettering. It had a common Christian cross to the upper left and a signet helmeted head with a round laurel surround to the upper right. It read as follows:

RICHARD I BONG
MEDAL OF HONOR
MAJ US ARMY AIR CORPS
WORLD WAR II
SEP 24 1920 · AUG 6 1945
DST SVC CROSS · SILVER STAR

I stared at this for quite awhile. I did not know anything about this man at this time in my life. However, I did have a superficial knowledge of "Medal of Honor". Enough to know this had been a man of importance. To the left, the next grave over I noticed another stone also flat to the ground. It read: Marjorie Bong Drucker 1923–2003. The grave site itself appeared to be fairly fresh. Probably within the last year. Little did I realize then the stories that would unfold. What I did do was make a mental note to look into this Bong guy. With that in mind I got back on my bike and continued with my day of leisure. Not knowing then, that in the days to come, I would meet the grave site visitor and begin the most wonderful summer of my life.

The 475TH Fighter Group

Here at the beginning of this narrative I would like to touch on the origin of the 475TH Fighter Group. The old pilot storyteller was a member and proud participant in that organization.

The 475TH group was formed in May 1943 at Amberly Field in Australia. By Aug they were operational and initially staged out of strips around Port Moresby, New Guinea. The squadrons operated here briefly while awaiting the finishing of the Dobodura airdrome complex. By the end of August this transition had taken place and they began to prosecute the war from there. It was a total P-38 Lightning unit and its pilots were culled mostly from pre-existing front line units. Some of them were fresh arrivals and quite a few had been in theater several months. Of the three squadrons the 431ST, the 432ND and the 433RD the 431ST squadron would produce a constellation of exceptional performers. These were *Satan's Angels*. They painted their prop cones and tail trims red and *Hades* became the call sign of the 431ST.

As a fighter group this would become the only fighter group in the world that flew the P-38 uninterrupted until the conclusion of the war. As such they became an endorsement of the P-38 being the best fighter of the war. Before it was over they would shoot down 551 enemy aircraft and individually they would achieve spectacular results along with sometimes painful tragedy. Let me now introduce you to some of the top performers who flew with or in the squadrons of the 475TH Group. Major Bong, Major McGuire, Charles Lindbergh just to name a few. All three squadrons produced great Aces and great stories and in the end the 475TH Group did a magnificent job collectively prosecuting the air war. However, my association deals primarily with the history and combat exploits of members of the 431ST Satan's Angels. What follows will be the best that I can recall as factual as I can tell it. My story is based on combat reports of actual engagements, eye witness accounts and my personal experience. I have spent the summer telling all this to an interested young man in the community whom I met at my favorite fishing spot. He in turn took it upon himself to transpose my story into book form. I hope you enjoy the narrative. Let us now begin.

Recollections of my Uncle

I am Reena, I am now 28. I enter here to tell the Japanese side of the story. I am a University student in my final year of a masters degree. This is the story of my Uncle and his participation in the Pacific War. Some of the story is based on his conversations with me and a lot of it has been drawn from his personal diary. It begins at a lawn party to see him off to the war in China in 1937. At times the story will be related as best it can in the form of first person recall. At other times it will be told in the manner of second hand recollection and lastly there are parts that are relayed through a composite personality. The last to protect the names of some individuals unfortunately consumed by the war but, nevertheless persons whose stories and experiences were indelible to my uncle and relevant to the experiences remembered. Although there are fictional sequences the historical occurrences are accurate and factual as well as can be portrayed. It should be noted my uncle having been born in 1915 was 80 years old when he began to talk to me of his activities in the Imperial Japanese Navy. I was just 15. He died in 2003 at the age of 88 and gifted to me his personal diary of which I knew nothing until his passing.

Uncle passed in the winter and as I was involved mid semester I waited until spring break to study his diary. I chose a fine spring day in the nearby seaside park at Hamadera near Osaka. There in the warmth of the sun, beneath a canopy of fresh cherry blossoms on a park bench I opened the diary and quickly leafed through it front to rear. I then went back to the very first entry Aug 1931. "Today I entered into the service of the Emperor. I reported to boot camp for my initial training in the Imperial Japanese Navy etc, etc..." I then moved to the last page and worked backward to what much to my surprise turned out to be a very long narrative summation of the preceding entries. As I began to read I found it was about other people as well as major events and that it was almost like a book. It started around the beginning of the Pacific War and ended in August of 1945. It went something like this:

On a small plot of ground in the paddies of Osaka Prefecture a family knotted themselves to well wish and say goodbye to their eldest son Bano. He was a recently graduated 21 year old Imperial Japanese Navy fighter pilot. It was 1937 and their son was leaving for the war front in mainland China. He was a Navy pilot but, his Sentai would be active in supporting Army ground combat in the Shanghai area as well as interdicting the aerial forces of the Chinese Government. There was an Uncle in attendance in addition to close family members. The Uncle had served aboard a Navy destroyer at the Battle of Tsushimah in 1906. It was he who had pushed Bano to seek a career in the modern Navy.

He looked very sharp in his white dress uniform and it was clear both his Uncle and his immediate family members were proud of his achievement. Here he was Zero Naval fighter pilot. It had been a long hard journey but, well worth the effort. Again, it was Uncle who saw the future and encouraged him to become a Naval aviator. As they talked a woman stepped from the adjacent farm house and slowly picked her way along the narrow paddy trails that led to the nearby farm to city road. She was petite and shapely beneath her tight slacks. However, it was the sway that caught his eye rather than the shape beneath the pants. She moved sensuously on this most mundane rice paddy journey and he could not help but notice. Soon she was out of sight, off to the train and back to the big city. It turned out she was a cousin of the neighbors, had never been here before and it would be many years until he saw her again. Still, the scene and her image would visit him often in the years to come sometimes even in battle. In time they would be introduced and a wonderful and enduring relationship would follow but, not today. It was time now for him to bade them all farewell. He saved the last goodbye embrace for his frail mother. He hugged her gently and promised as all good sons do to return. She was heavily arthritic but, had a will of iron. She in turn hugged him as tightly as she possibly could, reluctantly broke the embrace and then he was gone. As he threaded his way along the narrow paddy trails she stood and waved until he was out of sight.

It was a glowing moment for him and thus he recorded it in detail. It was then a happy time in Japan and his career and his mothers waving farewell stayed with him even as an elderly man.

There then follow some entries dealing with his early missions and first success as a fighter pilot against the Chinese forces. It is part of his story yes but, the real story begins when he was assigned to the New Guinea combat theater in early 1942. Flying mostly out of the great base at Rabaul he flew against every major target area from Guadalcanal to Port Moresby to the far Western reaches of New Guinea. The Guadalcanal entries are sparse and short. Mostly abbreviated times and dates as the activity was intense, he was young and often exhausted at days end. By late '42 Guadalcanal had been lost and the battling shifted to our New Guinea stronghold. Here he hit his stride as a mature, experienced fighter pilot and his story begins to unfold with insight and definition rather than terse entries.

Please to join me now as we follow the flying adventures of my great Uncle and his fellow flyers as he served Emperor and country in the great Pacific War. The first diary entry begins with:

I came to New Guinea in early '43. All through '42 we had

dominated the air war here however, we could not dislodge them from the toe hold at Moresby. It all began to change when the Lightnings showed up. They were few in number only a squadron or two until about August. Even in low numbers they were a dangerous foe and worse, they could stay with the bombers now reaching our distant bases at Wau and Hollandia.

That's why my unit was sent there. When it began to turn the authorities strengthened the base defense with Navy units. The Army boys were good don't get me wrong. There just were not enough of them plus, they were not as good at flying long distance over water. One day in August stands out in particular. It was one of those exhilarating moments in life that you never forget and you relish retelling until you are an old man.

My buddy Irumi, "The Demon," had force landed some days ago in the Admiralties. His aircraft was junked but, the Army had an Oscar headed to our base so, he strapped it on and headed back home. It was a clear balmy day, he was in no hurry so, he putted back with the canopy open at 500 feet and 200 MPH. He said later it was the most relaxing flight of his life that is until just near Saidor out over Markham Bay he flew into a squadron of P-38's returning from a mission West of us.

In our huts and on the flight line we could hear the drone of the approaching squadron and we tumbled to our defenses fully expecting attack. The attack took place out over the bay when eight of them went after Irumi not us. The other eight circled at a distance as the contest began. Irumi was smart he stayed low to the water. The nimble little Oscar was at its best in the thick air close down. The Demon went to work as only he could. He turned and rolled, slipped and jinked and even got in a couple of tight loops. He split S'd a lot and his chandelles baffled them when he would fall off on a wing and let the lift dynamics spin him right back into them. He was so good it was almost like the erratic descent of a falling leaf.

On the flight line we stood transfixed. We did not attempt to join him he was pulling the whole show toward the base. We knew they would quit at landfall to avoid our anti-aircraft guns. He would either make it or he wouldn't. I could scarcely breath as I watched probably the most thrilling aerobatic demonstration ever. I knew in my heart he was good enough and eventually, my faith rewarded, the Americans broke off and headed for home.

A few minutes later Irumi pulled up on the tarmac, canopy still open, looking as if he had come from a walk in the park. There was not one hole in the little fighter. He then spent a few minutes describing his tactics to the young pilots and after the crush of congratulations subsided he went to our tent for a well deserved nap. When he awoke after supper he and I had a good laugh about the whole incident.

That night the neophytes howled until after midnight vicariously reliving the almost magical display they had witnessed that afternoon. That was the beginning of the legend of The Demon. To this day it is my favorite remembrance from the time of the war. It is one of the very few bright moments of the war and alas, I am getting ahead of myself.

Let us back up now and let me revisit the very first time I saw a Zero fighter plane. The Zero, "the sword of the Empire."

There it was sitting gracefully in the early afternoon sun. As I walked around it for the first time ever I could not help the rush of pride and excitement. It was thin, and lite, nosed with a huge and powerful air cooled radial engine and elegantly aerodynamic. Two 20 MM cannons in the nose and 13.7 MM machine guns in the wings promised a deadly sting. Poised on its tail wheel nose in the air the big red roundel logos gave it an air of authority. This was all reassuring but, it was in the air that I was seduced. At a little over 5,000LBS and nearly 1,000 horsepower its performance was stunning. It was fast and lithe and so aerobatic it could be made to flit about almost

like a moth. When called upon it was fast for its day yet eco-
nomical giving it the range to strike distant complacent targets never dreaming it would show up.

In the period 1939-41 it was almost like a secret weapon.
Westerners who did hear about its performance refused to believe it. It was that far ahead of everything else. In skilled
hands below 10,000 feet it could almost turn on its self. It
was just a joy to maneuver. The fliers embraced it and put
it to work with immediate reward. All up and down the Asian
perimeter the Zero in its many different guises dominated the
air battle wherever it occurred. It could be beaten but, only
with hit and run attacks on the unsuspecting. Any time it was
engaged in a dogfight the other guy typically lost. That was the
Mitsubishi A6M Zero...pound for pound the best fighter plane
in the world 1941.

Then there were the men who flew it. We were young, we
were confident, we were at the beginning of the Pacific War
the best trained fighter pilots in the world. We were imbued
with Bushido and the aura of the samurai. The Japanese Imperial Navy was the largest fleet in the world and we led aircraft carrier innovation. We had fourteen aircraft carriers to
Americas four. All of them staffed to perfection with highly
trained handling crews. We were without question the best
weapon in the Japanese inventory.

We came to the eve of battle with probably the best aerobatic combat team since the Lafayette Escadrille in WWI. With
an average of 700 hours of flight training before being introduced to carrier operations we were superb masters of our
task. After carrier certification most of us saw combat duty
in the China theater from 1937 on. Thus we came to the contest with what was at the time the finest and most dangerous
fighter plane in the world. By the dawn of "The day of Infamy"
many of us were already combat Aces. We knew our aircraft
intimately, we were trained to the game and we were dedicated and fearless. We were "the sword of the Empire".

Kelly Johnson: Michelangelo of the Air

I guided my bike down off the highway and onto the dirt path leading to the parking lot. A few yards further on I came to rest next to where the old man sat fly rod in hand angling the stream. We exchanged hellos as I leaned forward chest pressing the cross bar, panting. It felt good leaning into the bar both feet flat on the ground. I hung like that for quite awhile gently rocking the bike frontward and backward until my normal breathing resumed. After a bit the old man asked. "Ridin' pretty hard there sonny"? "Yea, I was really given it there the last couple of blocks...it felt good" I replied. Well I'll tell you what son. Now that you have collected yourself I'm going to talk to you today about the most wonderful airplane of the war and the great man that designed it." With that he motioned me to sit down on the big log next to his lawn chair. As I sat and adjusted to my comfort he began to speak.

We are going to talk for a while about a man named Clarence "Kelly" Johnson. Kelly Johnson is without question the greatest aircraft designer to have ever lived. Beginning in his early 30's as an employee of the Lockheed Aircraft Company in Burbank, California Kelly demonstrated his aircraft design genius when tasked to the fighter that would become the P-38 Lightning. Let's go back to a Government directive issued in Jun 1937. It was decided the US would need a "Pursuit" aircraft suitable to stop the anticipated advance of heavy bomber warfare. Over at Lockheed the young visionary was assigned the responsibility along with Bill Hillard to meet the government objective. Let's touch on this seeming dual effort. It is pretty well recognized by those who study these things that this was a Kelly Johnson effort with Bill assisting as a system administrator but, that Kelly was the aircraft designer. Having stated that, what he rendered was nothing less than revolutionary.

Kelly thought deeply about how to exceed performance as initially envisioned. He knew and understood the current palette of technology at the time. He looked at the parts bin, wrapped his thoughts into exceptional performance and designed an air frame that went way beyond the mission statement. Right off the top he created a firing platform. He resolved the convergence zone problem inherent in wing mounted guns by setting them in a pod in the nose thus making the plane a point and shoot weapon. This also extended the effective bullet contact range to 1,000 yards as opposed to the 250-300 yard limits of convergence zone wing mounted weaponry. He doubled the engines for power and pilot safety. He saw that it would need to reach out to the enemy so, he made it large that it could carry more fuel. He then sleeked the aircraft to its power potential and placed it on a tricycle landing gear for ease of landing and taxiing. As the airplane evolved his genius for aeronautics became apparent. It was fast, *maneuverable*, had *vicious* point and shoot firepower, and it had very long range for the day. This and the redundancy of power made it an aggressive offensive weapon rather than a defensive one as originally envisioned.

When it arrived on the eve of battle it was a stunning piece. All that was then needed was to train men to the tool. Kelly Johnson took the best of everything that propeller technology had to offer and shaped it into an elegant, deadly fighting machine. With his exceptional vision he took the prop driven fighter to the edge of what the jet fighter would become. It is probably the best all around aircraft of the prop fighter era and certainly the most striking profile of the century. The men who flew it in the Pacific loved it. Beyond all of its flight performance capabilities was the constant assurance that with two engines one of them would bring you home and it did. Time after time over vast reaches of open water and great stretches of hostile jungle...it would bring them back to base camp. You just can't emphasize that enough. One airplane in particular did this five times!

In a way he kind of slipped one over on the brass but, it was a positive con job not a harmful or self serving one. The Army thought they wanted a small, light, short range, interceptor that would rise quickly above threatened cities to knock down heavy bombers. What he gave them was a fighter 100 MPH faster than they thought feasible and a performance envelope almost beyond their belief. When the P-38 arrived it was the first airplane to fly to 40,000 feet. It was the first military aircraft to break 400MPH. It was the first to employ flush rivet construction, stainless steel structural components and flush butted aluminum panel fitment. It was the first duty fighter with tricycle landing gear. It was a big airplane. At roughly 14,000LBS it was 3 times bigger than the average WWII fighter. Remember, he made it big to carry fuel. Ultimately it would fly missions of 9 hours and 2,000 mile duration with loiter and fight time included at the contact point. This was unheard of in the late 30's. At only 180 MPH and 30 degrees pitch it would out climb any other Axis prop fighter. This was important, Kelly designed this into his fighter. Opponents would have to pitch nearly vertical at full power in an attempt to match it and they would soon stall out and fall off the hunt. It would climb steadily like this from ground to 10,000 feet in eight minutes. It was phenomenal performance for the period and would not be matched until jets began to mature. Only Kelly Johnson saw these things as a concept. He literally could see what the aircraft was going to do in his mind and then he rendered it through industrial genius. That was the P-38 and that was Kelly Johnson the Michelangelo of aeronautic design, fall 1941...on the eve of battle.

When he was done talking of these things I asked a few questions which he obligingly answered...he always took the time to answer my queries no matter how trivial or ignorant. Later as I got older I appreciated this more than I did at the time. He was teaching me, patiently teaching me while educating me about that which he knew best. Pretty soon he indicated he had caught enough supper for himself and his wife.

As he began to pack things up I kicked my bike into action and headed for home. As I pedaled on toward home I thought about what he had just told me. That last phrase kept going through my head, "The Michelangelo of the Air". I of course had heard of Michelangelo and I knew by now about the fabulous P-38 fighter—*The Michelangelo of the Air*. As I coasted into the driveway I made a mental note to hit the computer and look up this Johnson guy...I had never heard of him before today.

The new Richard I. Bong Veterans Historical Center on the shore of Lake Superior, City of Superior, Wisconsin.

The "Kid" From Poplar

Let me tell you about Major Bong. This was a man from "Gods Country". That's what the folks around his hometown call it. Richard was born and raised on a small farm near Poplar, Wisconsin. This is a beautiful area in the far north of Wisconsin and just to the West of the great lake Gitcheegoomee as the Indians call it or, Lake Superior on your geographical maps. It is an out of the way place with rambling forests and a multitude of outdoor recreational opportunities. Winter though harsh, almost hostile, can have a crystalline beauty especially after fresh snow and sub zero temperatures. Spring time is exhilarating, the summers are lush and typically cool while the fall is pure enchantment. In his free time Richard would roam, hunt and play in this almost magical wonderland of forest, lakes and streams. Nearby Bayfield County and the adjacent off shore Apostle Islands National Park were great for deer hunting or summer recreating. From this tranquil milieu came Americas greatest technological hunter. The soft spoken, stocky, and deadly proficient sky warrior Richard Ira Bong.

I began to fly with Richard as soon as he arrived in Sep of '42. It was clear from the start, he loved the '38 and he was at home driving it. He began actual combat flying sometime in Dec and it didn't take him any time at all and he was an Ace. Seven or eight weeks, something like that. Not long after that he was a "Double Ace" and so it went. Here's the important part. Maj. Bong was yes, proud of doing his job but, there was no bragging, no strutting, for him it was a job. His was a mission to vanquish the offender and protect all that was good about America.

He was a very good pilot and he was courageous beyond the norm. In the beginning he felt he was not that good at distance shooting so, he would fly up very close to them that he could not miss and then he would stay on them until he cut them down. Once Bong was on your tail there was no getting away. I know, I tried many times in mock combat, I could not shake him. It was almost like he had a sixth sense about what they would try to do to evade him. Conversely if they got behind him he would utilize the P-38's attributes to get away by climbing or diving. He never personalized combat even when his friends were killed. There was no vengeance, just a consistent, methodical, professional effort.

On the ground he kept to himself. I mean he wasn't a recluse...he was a quiet man. In the early years he did not smoke, would only have an occasional drink and played very good baseball and a fair clarinet. Most people don't know this...he was a very good singer. He sang even in the church choir back home and Marge told me he would often sing to her.

Richard was always fearless and never reckless. Once I saw him fall in behind a shot up fellow pilot struggling to get home on one engine. To help the stricken pilot Richard fell in behind him and cut one of his own engines off and feathered the prop to draw the Japs off the other bird. How selfless does it get? It worked too. Next thing you know he's bagged one that fell for the ruse. Meanwhile the fellow he helped made it back to safety. How many other guys would stick their neck out like that? I never saw anyone else do it.

We flew all over the place from Moresby, and Dobo all the way up and down the Eastern coast of New Guinea, over the Owen Stanley Mountains, down through the Markham Valley. Once we locked in at Dobodura we went to the outer islands. The Admiralties, up to Rabaul, the Balikpapan oil fields...that was a nine hour ride with plenty of fighting once we arrived. You name it, we went there. Back up and down New Guinea again...the Battle of the Bismark Sea. We destroyed a whole fleet and a replacement army there. Finally we drove them completely out.

They had left Guadalcanal by then and we began to really take them on at the big complex at Rabaul. All through late October and into November of '43 we went up there every day the weather allowed. Bong was off to the states for a awhile for a well deserved rest but, soon enough he was back and running the score up some more. Getting back to Rabaul. We would escort the bombers. The targets would alternate between hitting their air bases and attacking the ships in Simpson Harbor. Always there were big air battles. They would send up every zero they had 50 and 60 at a time and the flak was heavy everywhere. They were very good with anti-aircraft fire. They were fearless, they would stand their ground and shoot back when you ran on them.

That's how Tommie Lynch got it. He and Bong had become friends and tent mates plus they had been given liberty to fly when and where they chose. That's how he would wind up flying with us even though he was not assigned to the 431ST. Anyway Tommie and Dick were on a hunt when Tommie was shot down. Lynch was as good as Bong and at the time of his shoot down he was ahead with 20. He had leadership skills beyond the norm.

Lynch was at that time the Wing Commander. Having gone on an unsuccessful hunt these guys decided to strafe some coastal shipping barges near Atape. It is believed one of them was heavily fitted with anti-aircraft weapons and on a second pass they found the range and knocked Tommie down. Bong watched helplessly as Lynch ejected from his exploding fighter only to have his parachute fail to deploy as he streamered to his death in the jungle below. As Richard explained it—he saw him free of the cockpit but, as he fell

Thomas Lynch, Bong's Good Friend who was KIA at Atape in 1944 by fierce anti-aircraft ground fire

to earth his chute never opened—he was too close when he jumped plus his flaming aircraft blew up beneath him. It was a sad day for Richard, as they had become close friends. As it was Dick was lucky to get home himself. He had to feather an engine shortly after and the running one had holes in the oil lines. He had over 80 bullet holes in his aircraft. Very lucky indeed.

That's a good enough introduction for today son. We'll get back into this another day. There is a lot more to tell you about. Don't worry we're going to cover it all. Just be patient. Right now I've got to get back up to the house my wife will be expecting me to take her to supper. I watched the old man rise and head for his waiting car rod and tackle in hand. As he opened the trunk to his Buick I spun my bike around and headed back to our place. Mom would be expecting me home for supper. As I sped down the country lane my head fairly spun with visions of the information I had so recently received. Right after supper I planned to hit the computer. At that time I did not know much about Richard Bong but, I was about to learn, enough probably to write a book.

Goodbye to Mom...Salute to Sebring

As he saw me approach and dismount from my bike the old man greeted me with "Hello son and good afternoon to you". I then replied "and good afternoon to you sir" followed with "have you caught any today?" He then replied "As a matter of fact three so far. One more and there will be a meal for me and the Misses." He then invited me to pull another lawn chair from the trunk of the Buick and to join him as he repositioned his chair further back in the shade of the overhanging tree. I sat down and watched as he carefully re-baited his hook and fed the line back out into the lite current. He was fishing for brook trout and he was using a very lite line and leader. He was letting the bait float just beyond where the rocks made the stream cavitate. There was a fair sized hole that had been chewed out by the constant churning of the water. Just the place a hungry brook liked to hang looking for an easy meal.

Satisfied with the set of the line he eased himself back into his lawn chair while grasping the rod in one hand and as he looped his right index finger under the filament and drew it to early warning pressure he turned to me and said. "Today I'm going to introduce you to Thomas B. McGuire son". "Right from the top, so you can maintain your attention...and I'll call him Tommie most of the time from now on." "Tommie was our number two Ace of all time with 38 confirmed combat kills". "So you can see right off he was basically the equal of Major Bong but, nonetheless fell short of passing him and for a reason that we will get to in time but, I'm getting ahead of myself so at this point we will back up and start all over." Tommie wasn't reckless like a lot of people like to claim. He was measured, confident, very smart and a natural pilot with flying skills way beyond even highly qualified test pilots. Yes, he was, cocky but, when you can back it up with performance, so be it. I'll begin Tommies story with an early career flying event he was fond of describing. I will relate it as close as I can to how he would have explained it.

First of all, he looked a lot like Errol Flynn a very famous movie star from the period. He had the same thin mustache, you see it in all the photos. He was thinner than Errol by probably 25 lbs. Tommie probably never weighed over 140 in his prime. He always wanted to be a pilot even before the war began, that was his ambition. When he finally completed all his training and was about to ship off to war he determined to say goodbye to mom and his hometown of Sebring, Florida in a very special way.

So, we have this Errol Flynn like character, on the ground but, not in the air. That was a whole different ball game and this able aviator was about to strap on his war machine and prove it. With that thought in mind he fired the big Allison and after warming it to spec he pointed his slim, modern fighter into the wind and ascended into a clear blue Florida sky. Today would be good bye to Sebring, good bye to mom day. He had something very special in mind for them all.

Quickly he rose to 3,000 feet and pointed the nose North toward Lake Jackson, and Sebring. Arriving overhead a few minutes later he circled Lake Jackson and brought his craft low to the water on the South end of the lake and at about 80% power he guided it North at just above tree top starting at the intersection of Lakeview and N Ridgewood Dr. Approaching 50 feet off the ground at 350 MPH he hauled back on the stick a block away from the flag pole and the hot P-40 was straight up and climbing hard as he passed inches above the chrome pole cap. In his wake the big oaks shook while chewed up leaves swirled in the air before floating back to earth. Rising to 3,500 feet he rolled all the way through a loop bringing himself back down to the tree line on the opposite side of the flag pole. From there he ran another mile at tree top down Ridgewood then banked hard over Dinner Lake and headed West toward his base at Orlando next stop for rest on his way to his next assignment. Lt Thomas B McGuire fresh fighter school graduate on his way to war. Little did he know...he would never see his hometown or his mother again. On the ground a lot of people probably guessed who it was ...nobody complained, they watched in awe as the P-40 sped off to the West at tree top height. That was Tommie McGuire April of '42.

He did some time initially in Alaska for about a year and then finally he was sent to the Pacific where he flew a little with the 49TH and then very quickly was assigned to the 475TH Group when it formed up. They got going in August of '43 and by Oct he was a double Ace. One day around then in a big battle over Oro Bay he knocked three of them down real quick and then got shot down himself. They put some bullets and shrapnel into his body as well as his airplane and he had to bail about 25 miles out to sea. A PT boat saw him arguing with them and picked him up right after he hit the water. They said it happened so fast that the last two planes he shot down and his were all three falling at the same time.

Tommie got three Distinguished Flying Crosses and a Silver Star in his first eleven days with the 475TH and another DFC, two Air Medals and a Purple Heart within his first two months and 13 Japanese confirmed. No one will ever match that record. He took on seven of them by himself that day and shot three of them down. He was noted for that, Tommie was fearless. He was always heading into groups of three or four of them. That's why he would shoot down two and three at a time. He was an exceptional flier, he wore that airplane like a skin. He could do things with those P-38s the test pilots never dreamed of. I've seen him bring those birds home with the wings bent, tail booms twisted, rivets popped out of the wing roots. He just knew how to push them farther than anyone else could.

I've seen him come back to base in a high speed pass on the runway, shut his engines off, pull up into a loop and extend the landing gear at the top of the loop and land dead stick. It was fun to watch, the plane would make this eerie whistling noise when he cut the engines. He'd then jump down and laugh as he hit the tarmac. Bong may have been a better shot but, Tommie was the best fighter pilot in the Pacific by far.

Well I guess that is enough for one day. That will give you plenty to think about for awhile. There is of course much more but we'll save that for next time.

With the story ended I nodded acknowledgement and as suddenly as I did that the string tightened on the old mans finger and grasping the rod with both hands he began to pull the line gently toward the shoreline. I could see the line cut toward the far bank against the tug of his rod. Very quickly the fiberglass rod began to bow at the end and as the old man pulled harder it began to bow even more until finally it began to quiver from the strain. He had a good sized fish going here, it looked to be bigger than the norm. Right about then it came out of the water in a burst of spray. It was big alright. The gullet was a good two inches deep and he was probably 16 to 18 inches long. This guy was going to dress out close to a pound. If he could land it. As the fish cleared the water it became clear it was not a brook, this was a German Brown and the battle was on. Three minutes later the fish was out of fight and the old man pulled him on shore and exclaimed "What a beauty supper is assured". Then he casually remarked "You can't believe how much I missed this two years off to war in the Pacific." With that he loaded up his catch and gear and we bade each other good bye until the next time. As the Buick hit the black top I turned onto the country lane and as I rode along I kept thinking about that last sentence and how he connected that long ago yearning with a right now occurrence and I still think about it occasionally even to this day. Later that night as I lie in bed close to slumber I kept going over the days conversation and I kept asking myself. How could a man fly so hard or so well he routinely bent his airplane without tearing it apart?

Dobo: The Hornets Nest

It was early July. We were enjoying the 4TH with lots of patriotism evident . The usual parade after which everyone gathered at the local Fireman's fund raising cookout at the local city park. As typical on the 4th I was told, the cloudy sky was low and threatening but, the rain held off until after dark. Everyone from babies to octogenarians seemed to be having a good time visiting with most consuming more beer than they needed and some overloading on ice cream.

The real hook for most were the old fashioned 100% beef burgers smothered the German way in fried sweet onions. Condiments were available but, most went straight onion . The buns were fresh and the halves were toasted face down in the same grease from the cooking burgers. If you didn't like burgers there were bratwurst cooked on the charcoal grills. They were cooked until they crackled when you bit into them. A lot of people ate them with raw diced onions and mustard. Either choice was out of this world.

That's where I ran into the old pilot. He's was sitting at a park bench with examples of both meats and some home made potato salad and a dab of baked beans on his plate. His wife had elected to stay home fearing rain. So, with my loaded plate I joined him. He said he came every year since the war ended because it was so good and he was thankful because he couldn't get food that good in the war zone. My first bite was into the burger and it oozed juice and blood and was out of this world. The bratwurst was equally tasty, crunchy and crusty like it should be. They didn't serve food like this back

29

in the big city. I wish they did.

We finished eating and the old man began to talk again of the war. Today I want to talk to you about Dobodura air field on New Guinea. Being part of it had been a big part of his life. I'll do my best to reconstruct what he said. Here is what I got from the conversation.

Dobodura

By January 1943 the decision had been made to build a new aerodrome complex at Dobodura. It was chosen because of its strategic location. The actual build site was on a vast kunai grass plain. It had a solid underlay to support the big bombers and it drained well to carry the torrents away and keep the aircraft in the air. When it was finished there were 11 different airstrips with interconnecting taxi-ways and aircraft revetments lined the edges. It was a huge, intricate complex with areas of maintenance, fuel dumps armament housings, living quarters and chow halls. It was a small city in the middle of nowhere and all supplies had to be brought in by air.

The aircraft were there by the hundreds. Whole wings of bombers, cargo ships, fighters, even the tiny liaison L-5's. The launch and recovery runways were made of solid, crushed and packed coral. They were so wide P-38 fighters would take off four abreast. Whole squadrons of sixteen aircraft would be up in minutes. It was something to see.

When they came back from bomb runs especially Rabaul many of them were heavily damaged. Often they would just make it back. Once I watched seven B-25's in a row crash land. They dug the guys out, doused the fires then bull dozed the remains to the side and left them there. They were our "Parts supply depot". Many, especially the fighters were picked to the bone. When the war ended in '45 there were over a thousand scrapped planes here even some Japanese ones that had been shot down over the area.

In its heyday, February '43 to December '44, it was a hornets nest to be sure. Combat aircraft just came and went all day long. Lots of them never returned. By the end of '44 Dobo was slowing down. The war front had moved beyond her reach. It was now centered around Biak and the Philippines and Dobodura had become a pass through on the journey to the front. Still in all its history is rich with our very best working out of there. Guys like Bong and McGuire, Kerby, Lynch, Donnie Roberts, McDonald, and lets not forget the great Gerry Johnson. Three of those seven earned the Congressional Medal Of Honor. It was like a training ground for Aces and a career touchstone for greatness. In its day Dobo was the counterweight to Rabaul. In the end we prevailed but, it was not easy and a lot of good men were sacrificed to gain the win.

New Guinea

It was the Stalingrad in the Pacific. The Japanese lost 350,000 men there and Dobodura was the spark plug. What a place. I wish you could have seen it...and then it was over...its importance irrelevant it slowly reverted back to jungle.

We each had another brat and called it a day. He went his way and I went home stuffed to take a nap. When I awoke it was after dark so I got on the computer and looked up "Dobo". Lots of info, lots of photos. That place was truly a hornets nest. The Japanese lost a lot of sleep over it but, to no avail. As the old man said in about a year it had become obsolete and after the war just returned to jungle.

Anyway, I enjoyed the food, the newly gained knowledge and the culture of the community up close. This is where Dick Bong came from. The small town of Poplar, 500 population even 60 years later. These are good people. This is what made Dick who he was.

Suddenly it was getting late. I'd had a great day and great

food. I snapped the light off and rolled into bed. Not long after the rain began to fall. I loved the drumming on the porch roof that ran past my bedroom. My stomach bubbling with bratwurst I soon drifted off to sleep.

A Dragonfly Named Oscar

I arrived at the fishing hole late in the morning. The old flier was set up at his favorite spot. He was eased back in his lawn chair line played out in the pool just below the shallow rapids. I think he may have been dozing when I arrived but, hearing my approach he had recovered and he certainly wasn't going to let me know. Of course it did not matter. Its part of the fun of fishing, people do it all the time. We exchanged hellos, he remarked he had not yet had a bite and I settled down on my favorite log a short distance from him.

It was one of those hot, humid, overcast days that happen only in the Midwest in July. To make matters worse there was not a breath of air. There was no rattle of leaf and twig, no swish of breeze or bending grass. It was so still you could hear the drone of insects above the light gurgle of the stream. Owing to the shade of cloud the insects were out in large numbers. Even the mosquitoes. Great swirls of them evident over the water from which they hatch. They gathered in puffy cloud like masses here and there and drifted slowly from side to side never straying more than a foot or two in any direction.

Life was rich around the shallow but, wide stream. In addition there were gnats, butterflies, even the occasional grass hopper lifting from bank to bank. Birds large and small pecked along the banks while some speared water life others artfully snapped unaware insects from the air. Into this kaleidoscope of life came a dragonfly. One of those bright green iridescent four winged mosquito killers with two big multi-lensed eyes. Other than the hummingbird they may be the most masterful of all flyers. In a few minutes I would get a demonstration of their skill. For now I watched as he flitted here and there in pursuit of his tiny prey. Now and then he would hover and sometimes even fly backwards for a short distance. Other than these two exceptions all of his flying emulated other flying creatures. Except, he was far better at it than the competition.

It was right about then the action began. Among the birds feeding along the river a finch had spotted the dragonfly working the middle of the river. Diving from a tree he set his wings and banked from the side to intercept his meal. A defensive side slip by the dragonfly took him away from danger as the finch sped by way too fast to cut back to the target. Immediately the dragonfly returned to his post about two feet off the river and resumed the hunt. Every now and then he would lunge nearer to the water in one direction or another. I think he was harvesting freshly emerging mosquitoes too hard to see at that distance. It was clear he was eating something, maybe gnats. They were there too.

The finch meanwhile had flown to a branch opposite, rested a bit and then commenced a fresh attack. Once again the dragonfly artfully dodged to the side and continued hunting. There were other birds working the air too. You could actually hear their beaks click together as they caught their victims. Even the finch would distract at times and grab an easy bite as he rolled away from the dragonfly. This was all very fascinating and I asked the old man if he was on to the action. "Yes" he said. "I am watching". As he said this a second finch took a pass at the dragonfly that once again dodged the attack. By the time he arched away the first finch had begun another swoop. Soon it was evident the two birds were working together to attack the dragonfly. Time after time he skillfully cut or sliced in a different plane to avoid capture. Much to our delight this went on for several minutes at which point a third finch joined the attack.

They tried every approach imaginable sometimes coming on two abreast while the third flew in from the opposite direction. No matter how the attacks escalated the dragonfly continually evaded them sometimes with lightning like bursts of speed. In between swoops and dodges the dragonfly would always return to the hunt. After a while the birds seemingly frustrated and maybe beginning to tire turned as a group and flew downstream. Left to himself the steadfast insect killer continued to harvest his prey from the insect cloud. We discussed this event the old man and I until he began to describe a similar circumstance that occurred during the war. In anticipation I slid to a sitting position on the ground next to the log grabbed a nearby strand of tall grass stuck it in my mouth and began to listen to another fascinating story. It went something like this.

"It was the summer of '43. I was flying then with Gerry Johnson's 49TH Flying Knights. On this mission we were escorting B-25 strafers. Their task was to fly low on the water and chew up small coastal barges supplying the inland Japanese Army garrisons along the coast. Our job was to fly high cover and protect the bombers. Somewhere around Lae, Finschafen about 25 to 30 Japs show up and we got into a pretty good dust up. As I recall we knocked down 10 or 11...took some holes in our ships but, didn't lose anyone."

"On the way back around Saidor out over Markham Bay we run into a single Oscar putting along by himself. This guy is flying along with his canopy open and let me tell you, he may have been the best Jap pilot ever. Eight of the 9TH Fighter SQ boys go after this guy while the rest of us circled and watched at a distance. What the hell...at eight to one you would think this would be over in a matter of seconds. This guy took it right down to the water where the air is thick and he all but turned that Oscar inside out. He would jink and bank and turn back into the attack but, always avoiding the head on. Everybody took turns at him and he just kept dodging just like that dragonfly. Ever so slowly he was pulling the whole show back toward land where heavy anti-aircraft fire surely waited. We didn't want any part of that but, even more telling. After 15 minutes of intense flying everyone was frustrated and getting tired. We just couldn't touch him. He and his ship were too good. We then rolled off *en mass* and flew home. We let him go because we had to, he was an exceptional pilot. We laughed about it later over beers. That was our 'Dragonfly' ".

Summer of '43

I left soon after and returned to my aunts home on the edge of town. As I rode along I kept seeing that dragonfly in my mind surrounded by a bunch of P-38 fighters. With imagination I was transposing the battle he had just described but, I didn't know what an Oscar looked like. As I pulled my bike into the garage I made a mental note to resolve this.

Later that night after supper I retired to my room. I then turned on the computer punched in Japanese Oscar and began to learn about the amazing Mitsubishi Ki 43 Oscar fighter plane. Even before I met the old flyer I knew of the famous Japanese Zero. It is a name synonymous with the Japanese war effort. The Oscar it turns out was the Japanese Army version of the famous Zero which is more commonly associated with the Japanese Navy. The Oscar was lighter, a little bit smaller, and even more nimble than its Naval counterpart. In addition more Japanese pilots achieved Ace in the Oscar than the Zero and the Oscars shot down more allied and especially more American aircraft than any other Japanese fighter.

After a bit I began to follow the threads and by three in the morning I had covered pretty much everything the Japanese put in the air right up through the jet in the waning hours of the war. I had no idea it was this involved. It was clear, I had a lot to learn and for the next two nights I buried myself in the files. Among other things I found that Zeros and Oscars were the scourge of the air, at least in the first 18 months of the Pacific War they were arguably the best fighter planes in the world. Without question the Navy pilots were the most proficient and the best trained anywhere. The Army pilots though not as rigidly selected and extensively trained as the Naval pilots were more experienced as many had been flying combat since 1931 throughout Manchuria and China.

Through the years in idle moments I have often envisioned this event. Basically what happened that day over Markham Bay was a man blended the capability of his aircraft with his ability to fly it in an exceptional display of the will to survive. It may have been the greatest flying exhibition in history played out and witnessed by only 17 people, With his own mortality as incentive this guy kept his head, pressed his skill and escaped certain death. While eight wolves circled, and eight pawed, one man flew his Oscar like a dragonfly.

The Demon

He was tall for a Japanese at five foot ten, slight as a twig with the energy of a lion. 25 year old Irumi from Otsu on the sea was unquestionably the best military fighter pilot Japan ever fielded. His daring beyond the pale, his talent almost beyond belief. His ability to force an airplane to his will deadly to all who opposed him. His flying was alternately described as *snake-like*, hypnotizing, magnetic, even frightening to many. Over and over again he would enter the fray against overwhelming odds of 4-5 to one. Carefully threading his way from one victim to the next he would bore in and emulate their movements until finally he would as he put it, "assassinate them." Well at least it was merciful. When he opened up on them he would be scant yards away and he often shot the pilot with a short burst.

However, as a military example he was a disaster. He had disciplined himself long enough to qualify and graduate as a Navy fighter pilot. After a couple of years duty in China he had become well known and widely respected for his abilities and his fearless accomplishments. By the time he arrived at Rabaul he was known throughout fleet command as a rare and valuable asset.

Even still he was a headache to his superiors as he drank and caroused to excess. Often he was not available at his squadron compound and inevitably he would be visiting the "comfort women," or a local bar, or both simultaneously. Frequently he would be passed out in an off base whore house when attack was eminent. Underlings would be dispatched to drag him back to the flight line where he would often throw up before boarding his aircraft. Staggering and stumbling he would crawl into his fighter and tear off into battle as if possessed. He was truly something to see and he was an inspiration to all especially the young who idolized him. By the time he arrived at Rabaul they set him and his girl friend up in a shack adjacent to the airstrip gate area and ran a field phone directly to the bedside so they could roust him in time to get airborne and defend the harbor. They even supplied him with a beat up old Ford to get out to his fighter quickly a distance of about 3 miles. Somewhere around our tenure at Wewak he had started getting tight with Renatta. Because of his performance they dragged her along with them until by the time they got to the Philippines it was automatic and they set him up again with the phone in an off base shack. It was highly irregular yes, but, he was our very best. He inspired the young and every time he rose into the air he knocked down the enemy.

He was from a rice paddy family near the sea and it was his intellect and high academic scores that got him into naval aviation. He was not however, smooth or sophisticated. He had a lot of country boy in him plus he was a social rascal and he was quick to resort to fists if challenged.

She was a whole wild story of her own. Born to a poor family on the West coast she had been orphaned at the age of nine and raised herself more or less like a rat until she was shang- haied at the age of 17 in 1942. Initially she begged for food and slept in cracks. By the time she was ten she was support- ing herself by selling things mostly stolen fish from the mar- kets by the docks. In '42 when the round up came for comfort women an old woman in the area who despised her arranged to have her scooped up as just another Korean heritage girl. With no one to defend or aid her she was packed onto a trans- port on its way to the New Guinea theater. Once arrived she was pressed into service but, had only been used a couple of weeks when Irumi showed up. If ever two people were meant for each other this was it. They were on fire for one another from the moment they met. As already covered he was loyal, a fearless inspiration to all and exceptionally good at his job. So, when he asked for some favors they were granted. Thus he arranged to have her separated from the herd and to have her follow him as the airfield front moved back.

When he met her she was flinty, as crude as a box of rocks and as tough as a pine knot. Physically, she was tall for a Japanese and at five foot six and 108 pounds she was a "willow" with beautiful straight black hair and a sharp angular face. Later by the move to San Juan Field on Negros she began to improve herself and her beauty became evident to all. Naked she was stunning and would easily have hypnotized any man in her presence. However, she saved it all for Irumi for by the time of the move to the Philippines she had come to understand that she loved him. It hadn't taken long for her to quell his lust for other women and he too had become one with her by the time of the move to San Juan.

His drinking she could not curb but, he never got violent or angry and he treated her very well drunk or sober. She did not press him about this behavior after all, not only was he good to her. He was the only person that had ever been kind or exceptional to her. In the end she was grateful to have him drunk or sober. Soon she took to waiting for him by the gate. Dressed as best she could, often with a flower in her hair she was the envy of all. That was my buddy Irumi 1943. We flew all over the Southwest theater together until I was wounded in late '43. When that happened I was out for most of a year recovering and I saw him only briefly upon my return summer of '44. He was eventually consumed in the intense fighting in the Philippines. She then returned to Japan, worked in a factory, never married, and died in her seventies.

Freaks Of War

Oddities and Tragedies

The spring had come and gone, June had deeply enriched the landscape and I had begun to figure a few things out. Personally I was beginning to adjust to this remote, quiet place. I now knew the roads and trails and I found I enjoyed the smell of pine when I hit the front yard every day. I had come to look forward to my visits with the old man and some of the locals would now wave or speak to me if I came near. Eventually with the help of some new found friends I had even found my way to the beautiful white sands on the shore of Douglas State Park.

We had just come off a couple days of rain and neither I nor the old pilot had been to the trout stream. I had decided today to go to the beach, get some sun, do whatever. There were a lot of people in the park. After a while I took a walk up the beach front and sure enough I ran into the old man sitting in a lawn chair facing the water. Of course I walked over to say hello. Actually I sat down on his Coleman cooler and we began to chat about how pleasant it was and how beautiful it is to look out over the water on a clear day. All the while he spoke with me he was kind of transfixed with his eyes steady out over the lake. I could sense he was beginning to revisit the events from the past so I fed the small talk along until suddenly he turned to face me and this is what he began to tell me. Like everything in life warfare generates its own share of bizarre and strange events. The following are short synopsis

43

of some that I witnessed and some that were common knowledge following their occurrence or were related directly to me
by those who lived them. I'll start with what was actually the
first combat kill in the Pacific chalked up to the newly arriving
P-38 fighter.

It was attributed to Lt. Bob Faurot flying out of Moresby on
a mission against the Jap base at Lae. Incidentally Faurot was
one of the few to get into the air at Pearl. Anyway it was the
26 Nov 1942 and as they made their bomb run coming in off
the sea Faurot let his 500 pound bomb go so early it fell into
the sea short of the runway. At that moment a Zero coming
up to contest them flew into the water column as it detonated
causing it to crash. Because it was air borne and witnessed
by others in the flight Faurot was given credit for the kill. Lt.
Farout was a very good pilot and a good squadron leader. He
was lost at the Battle of the Bismarck Sea March 1943.

There was an incident involving the great Major Bong that
is nearly as strange. On a flight over Ormoc Bay in October of
'44 Bong had rolled over in pursuit of a Japanese dive bomber
at a lower level. Just as he was about to shoot the fearful Jap
pilot released his 500 pound bomb in an effort to lighten his
craft and to speed away. The bomb then spun back into the
tail area severing the tail empennage and the aircraft now
uncontrollable augured straight down into the jungle and
exploded. It was felt he had released his bomb at too steep a
dive angle thereby causing the calamity. Again because there
were several witnesses, Bong was given credit for the kill.

You will at times come across accounts of this incident
claiming that Bong inadvertently knocked this airplane down
by releasing his drop tanks while the Japanese crossed under
him. The first is the official version, either one worked over
beer so, they both persist. Only a few minutes later Bong got
himself involved in an equally bizarre situation which now
follows.

Not far away and near the Masbate coastline Major Bong

banked to his fourth attack of the afternoon. Completing his attack in a near vertical pursuit he chandelled into a flat heading back out into open water. A few minutes later the temperature began to rise rapidly on the starboard engine. Following procedure he feathered the prop and shut the engine down. As he did this he called out to his wingman about his condition and recommended they return to base which they did.

A half hour later and safe back at Tacloban he joined his crew chief inspecting the damage. They soon found a bullet lodged in the radiator of the left boom. This is what had caused the overheat and end of mission. It was a US .50 caliber machine gun bullet exactly like the ones used in his aircraft. Major Bong's wingman never fired a shot and no other US aircraft were in the vicinity.

By some fluke of physics Major Bong had flown into the path of his own gunfire. Probably when he flattened out of the vertical attack he had caught up to the trajectory perhaps on its way back down. In a way Major Bong shot himself down. There would be no credit for this encounter and no kill count added to the fuselage tally. The incident would however, make for good conversation over beer at the O club. After all how many guys were good enough to shoot themselves down? Yes indeed, Major Bong was a very lucky man, at least that day he was.

Man-To-Man Forever

Then there is the mid-air at Rabaul in Nov of '43. Once again witnessed by many. Carl Plank leading Green flight into battle over Simpson Harbor turned into a descending group of Zeros and picked one out. This was a head on approach. Both planes pressed forward firing steadily at one another. Blev Lewelling doing the wingman's job stayed tight with Carl. In a matter of seconds at a combined closing speed of 600 MPH the distance waned rapidly. This incident is a statement in it-self of the intensity of the Pacific War. Neither pilot wavered. Both held their ground straight and level until they collided and vanished in an orange red fireball with but chunks and pieces falling away. In a micro second Plank was gone. In-credulous Blev flew on into the battle, he then had only him-self to worry about.

Trading Paint

The Legend Begins The great Tommie McGuire got into one of these head on attacks over Wewak Airdrome in Aug of '43. It was only his 2ND combat mission ever. After two success-ful kills McGuire went into a head on with a Zeke. Again, each held his ground while they steadily hammered away at one an-other. As they passed their left wing tips scraped McGuires going just under the enemy fighter. Fortunately, they were just off center from one another or else they would have ter-minally collided.

They had both taken a few hits. In fact the Japanese left the area damaged. When Tommie returned to base his ground crew found green paint smears on the upper side of his left wing tip and bullet holes in his airplane. That's how close it was...a matter of millimeters. By nightfall Tommies legend had begun with talk of three confirmed, a fourth flipped away on a coin toss and a steely effort to knock one down with his wing tip. I might add he received a Silver Star for this days work. In fact, he was eventually awarded three Distinguished Flying Crosses and the Silver for his first eleven days of com-bat. A fete never matched by anyone before or since and only because these two guys "Clicked Wings" and flew away.

The Fatal Maneuver

An eerie parallel yet entirely different event occurred over Sek Harbor near Alexishafen when Danny Roberts and his wing man Dale Meyer collided in pursuit of an enemy fighter. Danny being the exceptional pilot he was simply turned tighter after the enemy than his wingman anticipated. Failing to match the turn the trailing wingman drove his fighter right into Danny's side resulting in the loss of both pilots. Danny at that time was the leading Ace in the 475TH having shot down 15 of the opponent in less than three months. He had been a high school music teacher before the war began. This was witnessed by several fellow fliers also.

The Gasoline Rainbow

On a mid January '44 flight over Wewak Col. Johnson exploded a lone Ki-43 at a mid level altitude. Several thousand feet below Bill Runey in a lower covering flight looked up at that very moment to see the avgas cloud shimmering as a rainbow just before it ignited. This was a most unusual event and may never, ever repeat again.

Finally amongst the tragedies there are some humorous events. Two of which follow more or less as they were recalled over beers at the "O Club". The first one once again involved the famous Major Bong. On a rescue mission over a New Guinea lake Major Bong had agreed to fly cover while rescuers paddled out to a small island in the lake where a downed aviator awaited their arrival. While circling the lake Major Bong soon noticed a 20 foot crocodile approaching the rubber raft from astern and unknown to the raft occupants. Being an avid big game hunter Bong proceeded to wind his fighter into a low level high speed pass on the hungry prehistoric beast. One can only imagine what four

.50 caliber Brownings with armor piercing shells did to a 2,000LB crocodile. It is said the rescuers were as terrified of the unexplained strafing run as they might have been had they known of the crocodile.

Too Close For Friendly

The next situation involves at that time Major Gerry Johnson. Sometime in Nov of '43 somewhere over the Markham Valley Gerry managed to shoot down an Australian Boomerang mistaken for a Japanese fighter on a low level strafing run.

Major Gerry Johnson with his Austrailian kill flag.

As the stricken fighter passed him he realized his error and radioed it's position near Gusap Air Base to ensure the pilots rescue from Japanese ground forces. The Aussie survived with a minor injury but, on recovery "Came looking for the guy who shot him down". They found each other at the

"O Club" in Dobo and over beers became friends. About two weeks later Gerry was on a scramble to intercept an unidentified aircraft near Gusap. The aircraft turned out to be one of our B-25's. As Gerry approached near to it to say hello a trigger happy side bay gunner mistook his P-47 for a Jap fighter and laced it front to rear narrowly missing the cockpit. With the engine and hydraulics knocked out Gerry was forced to crash land at nearby Gusap airfield wheels up. From then until he became the 49TH Group Commander and much to the chagrin of Aussies in the area Gerry had an Aussie kill flag mixed in with the Japanese credits on the nose of his fighter. It is not recorded whether the bomber crew painted a US flag on the nose with their "kill count".

Ice Skates In The Tropics

The battle for Biak Island turned out to be much more difficult than originally planned. The Japanese had shipped in a division of tough experienced fighters from the Manchurian front. In the end it took three weeks of hard fighting in cave like dug in positions to secure the island. During a resurgence of Japanese energy half way through the effort 19 officers and ground crewmen of the 475TH were pressed into defense of our positions and were lost in the ferocity of the fighting. After it was over an inspection team found a large shipping crate in a warehouse at Mokmer with hundreds of clamp on ice skates. This is very near the equator. It seems bureaucrats are universal in irrational behavior even in a time of war.

The Sad Story of John McClean

John McClean came to the SWPA in early '42. He was a good kid, a good pilot and everybody liked him. He was a green 2ND Lieutenant. straight out of flight school when he flew in from Townshend with four other guys all fresh graduates. So, all the old hands worked with these guys to bring em along and see they survived long enough to know what they were doing. A year later only John had survived. By Sep of '44 John was an old hand who had flown all over the theater and was known to everyone. It was a beautiful fall day I was sitting on the deck of the O Club, beer in hand. This was the club we built out over the water that sat on stilts at Mokmer. I watched as John circled the field one time then took his '38 off shore and did two victory rolls right off the beach and straight into the water. Lots of people saw this happen. In his excitement he must have misjudged something. The engines sounded fine, John was a good pilot and he had bagged two this day. It was a proud moment for him.

He went in so clean there was barely a ripple and no splash, no wreckage, no oil slick. John just flew that '38 into his grave, I think about him sometimes even now. I can still see him going in. We'll never know if he died on impact or drowned in the deep. I think the latter. I think that plane is intact off shore with John still in it. I think he was flying it when it came to rest. After the war ended I took some time one day. Got the charts out and looked it up. There's a shelf right in that area where he went in. It's about 700 feet deep. Most unfortunate.

That's how it went son, day in and day out, like everything else in life there were days of tragedy and days of triumph mixed in with long periods of boredom and moments of exhilaration. As you can see war is not immune from oddities and freakish events. It just plays out on its own tapestry. Because it is a deadly game it consumes those who make mistakes or drop their vigilance.

It was the setting I'm sure that fired his recall of these events long ago. For just a little while he and I traveled back to the hut on stilts over the Bay at Mokmer and we relived the tales of the young men at the bar. That's how it was told to me while sitting on the white sands of Lake Superior.

The Letter That Lives

The "Spirit" In The letter...

When I found this in the diary there was a note of explanation attached to it. This is a letter Kenji wrote to his mother about a one man dogfight he participated in over New Guinea in late '43. It begins with my Uncles short explanation.

I of course heard the story the day it happened. We talked about it that night. But, I did not know of the letter until his mother passed in the mid seventies. She left instructions that it be passed to me as he had requested. It was a great pleasure to have received it so many years later. Every now and then I would pull it out and read it again. It would be almost as if we were together as on the day it happened. Here it is in its entirety.

I was flying alone. I was out test flying an AM6 Zero that had required repair. Everything seemed in order and as I headed back toward base I throttled back to conserve fuel while I leveled off at about 1,000 feet altitude. It was a pretty, blue sky day with huge puffs of cumulous forming at about 3,000 feet and rising to about 10,000 feet and about a half mile in diameter. To my right was the open Pacific and to my left the rich green coastal jungle of New Guinea. The occasional river would shine silvery in the sun and I thought to myself they resembled the veins on a hand as they rambled from the inland mountains, down through the valleys and out to sea.

I stayed vigilant, panning my head left to right with the occasional glance back and up. Always looking for the enemy. Suddenly I noticed a glint a good distance to my rear and higher at about 5,000 feet. That aircraft was flying on the same heading and very likely was not friendly. Quickly I made some adjustments to my engine to increase the performance but, held my course and speed. As he closed I could see it was a Lightning and he was alone. I had been up against them many times and I knew he would attempt a high speed diving pass. When I could make out the red spinners on his engines I shoved my throttle to war power and began a sharp rising bank to the right. He tried to adjust but, was moving too fast and soon shot past me and banked left as I pulled my turn around in an effort to get behind him. Because of his dive speed he came around in his circle as quickly as I did. A few seconds later we were out of our turns and approaching one another head on. As I snapped back into level flight I mashed the trigger just as the nose of the'38 lit up with flashes of flame. About a mile apart we were now closing on one another at a combined speed of about 600 miles per hour. It was all happening very fast and if I didn't maneuver quickly there was a high risk we would collide. At just the last moment we both raked our craft to the right to avoid collision. As we rushed by I felt I could have stepped from one wing to the other. It was just that close.

Game on, we chased each other around the sky in straining maneuvers each trying to get the upper hand. I had the more nimble aircraft, he had more speed. He could out climb me, I made a mistake and he was soon too tight on my tail. Concerned, I found my way to a rising cumulous. With the '38 now hot on my tail and tracers flashing by I dodged and entered the cloud. As soon as the cloud shrouded me I pulled straight up into its tower for 3,000 feet.

I then banked hard to the left and began a spiraling descent. In seconds I broke out the bottom in its shadow. Looking back I could see the '38 just out of the cloud, high to my right, and beginning a roll looking for me. He was heading away and I used the moment to head low on the water and up an estuary issuing from the jungle. The trees here were huge, 75 feet on average. They hid me well as I hugged the water and followed the natural meander.

I needed a break. I was soaked in sweat, breathing hard, and my adrenalin charged heart was pounding madly. My limbs ached from the rapid and "g" intense aerobatics we had so recently indulged. I throttled back a third and tried to relax while scanning the sky around me. My fingers actually tingled and my knees trembled slightly. Suddenly I was taken with a spiritual sensation. It was almost as if...*the spirit of the sword*...vibrated within me. Never in my life have I felt so alive. Slowly my breathing and my heart settled. I stayed alert. This guy was still around. He was probably near my age. The engagement had been just as demanding for him. He would be recovering also. This was not the time to let down my guard. Just as I became fully collected tracers shot past my right wing. I turned away to the left, looked back and there he was sliding to the right but still, turning left with me. I kept pulling hard left, now just above the trees. I knew his fighter could not match me and as I came around behind him he banked right while climbing.

I fired a short burst but, the big Lightning was too strong. I could not reach the advantage. He stayed just beyond my guns and soon entered the cloud. I followed and in seconds broke through behind him just as he dove to the jungle below. It went like that for another ten minutes. We were both very good, neither could line up for the kill. My aircraft had performed magnificently as did his. It never coughed or faltered and answered my every command but, I was suddenly running low on fuel and I'm sure so was he.

There are moments in life when the rules get chucked. This was one of them. We were exhausted again and found ourselves circling lazily opposite one another. Catching our breath we eyed each other warily. We were from different worlds but, still, comrades in the game. It was then I made a bold move. Sensing he'd had enough and that he was low on fuel too I turned inside his arch in a non threatening way and slowly approached him on his left. He understood, throttled back a little and assumed straight flight until we were abreast.

We gazed across at one another for a minute or so and he waved in a friendly gesture. I nodded my head, waved back and then made a signal indicating to go home. He understood, confirmed the signal and waved again. We were so close I could see the smile in his eyes. Then, ever so slowly we each dialed in a little opposite rudder. Soon our craft separated and we slowly arched apart until our backs faced one another and we each flew toward home.

Back at the base a quick inspection of my fighter revealed no holes but there was a scraped area atop my left wing with grey paint ground in from the head on with the American fighter. It had been that close. It was almost as if we had clicked swords to begin a duel. I had fought with these red spinner guys before. They are a tough, skilled opponent. I consider myself very fortunate to have survived this event.

Later that evening I relived this whole contest with my friend Saburo. He listened intently, chuckled a few times and at the end He remarked."You did the right thing Kenji. War is about killing Yes. But, in the end it is about letting live also." Then in a serious tone he related to me a similar event involving him at the Battle of Guadalcanal. He had diced it up with an American Navy pilot until near exhaustion. About then the Yank leveled off and quit fighting. When Subaro drew abreast he could see the man was weak and bleeding plus his airplane evidenced much damage.

After looking him over he had gotten back on the mans tail. When he began once again to riddle the stricken craft there was no attempt at evasion. Soon it started smoking, rolled, and began a descending spiral toward the jungle. He felt the man was either dead or severely wounded. Ever since when he thought about this he felt remorse. He wished he had flown away and left the yank to his fate, perhaps to survive if left alone. He was certain now he had unnecessarily caused his death.

As I lay in my bed late that night drifting toward sleep I recalled the strange feeling I had experienced with the...spirit of the sword. My body first stiffened, then shuddered with the remembrance. It was a wonderful feeling to end a wonder filled day.

By now you have finished the letter. What a pleasing present it was to receive so many years removed from that time. To hear it again in his own words. We were all young then, in our prime. Kenji did not survive the war. He was consumed in one of the great battles over Luzon. He was a good man and a loyal friend. I miss him. Do not forget him. See to it he is remembered unto the generations.

Here then is the story of one day in the life of one of my Uncles flying buddies. Not being a "warrior" I can not feel the *spirit of the sword* as Kenji felt he did. But, after reading this letter I feel I know the spirit of Kenji.

Looking Back...Fall of '44

I found this more or less about two thirds of the way through the diary. It appeared to be a summation, or a reflection on the progress of the war up until the focus on the Philippines in the fall of 1944. There are notes, scratch outs and rewrites here and there. So, it appears that he wrote this then, but, re-visited it in later years and made changes, perhaps because with the passage of time he understood some things better. For example, the comparison of the P-38 fighter performance envelope to that of jet aircraft to come.

The commentary is broken into three phases and it begins in the immediate period right after the attack on Pearl and the occupation of the Philippines. With Phase 1 ended things quickly shifted to the Battle of Guadalcanal and New Guinea. Phase 2, the contest for what is commonly known as the Southwest Pacific Theater [SWPA] battle area had begun, it is as follows.

New Guinea was the next important real estate and the area from Rabaul to Port Moresby to Lae formed a large, crude triangle of death. At the start of 1942 we controlled all of New Guinea except for the Allied, mostly American toe hold at Port Moresby. Take that and the rich resources of Australia would be ours. In '42 the Zero was master of the sky. We owned the skies over that territory The Americans battled hard with their P-39's and P-40's but, they were no match to our Zero. Still they clung to that small complex of air bases and courageously fought us for every inch. Even in their weak position they launched offensive raids against our air bases. They drove their fast twin engine bombers daringly at tree top precision and caused us many losses of men and equipment. All throughout the spring of '42 and into the summer we prevailed. Starting in the late fall of '42 and early '43 things began to change quickly.

With the arrival of the "Big Lightning" we began to suffer noticeable losses. The P-38 flew higher, much faster, and it had greater range. It was agile for a big fighter and its cluster of heavy guns in the nose gave it point and shoot authority that could easily cut a Zero in half in seconds. Although not as able in a turn as the Zero the P-38 could readily dive away or out climb it.

Probably even more important, the American combat tactics had matured. Number one they emphasized team-work. They used two plane attack formations so the trailing plane could guard the attack aircraft. The lead man being pre-occupied with targeting it gave him confidence in his personal safety. Number two the Yanks were fond of methodical hit and run attacks. The impetus being a steady attrition of the enemy. It was a planned wearing down of our numerical strength to below our industrial and training capacity.

The 40,000 foot ceiling of the P-38 gave them the high ground. Typically combat took place below 20,000 feet as our planes functioned poorly above that level thus, of necessity, we stayed lower. Third, with some exceptions, for the most part they would not "Dogfight" us. Preferring instead to slash through our poised formations and dive or climb away at high speed.

The P-38 was the first 20TH century fighter. It evinced all the parameters of what would become the jet age fighter. It represented the epitome of prop age propulsion right at the end of its relevance cycle. Because of its superiorities it illuminated the change in tactics to a new level of aerial warfare. The great Ace Major Bong worked these tools and principles methodically and because he did it skillfully he became Americas greatest Ace and survived combat.

So it was by the end of '42. Yes, we had suffered a major loss at the Battle of Midway and the struggle at Guadalcanal was ending badly too. But, we still controlled 13 million square miles. An area rich in strategic resources and three times larger than Hitler's conquests. Even still, '43 was a more pivotal year and it began poorly with the telling loss of Adm Yamamoto 18 April at Bougainville. It was the Lightning that made it happen. That and the application of the afore mentioned tactics. This was a text book example of coordinated teamwork with utilization of all of the Lightning's attributes to accomplish this mission. Thus began the second phase of the Pacific War. 1943 the Southwest Pacific Theater was a tumble down year. It would be a long, tortuous, and agonizing string of defeats with some occasional successes forestalling the careful march of inevitability. Following the Yamamoto attack we suffered the disaster at the Battle of the Bismark Sea. The Markham Valley over central New Guinea became a hot bed of air combat. They came at us like clouds of hornets from the great base at Dobodura and they defended it fiercely. Every time we attacked there they cut our bombers down. Our fighter boys always fought bravely. We got our licks in but, more and more we were having to use young, poorly trained and vastly inexperienced pilots. The attrition was embarrassingly high.

They knocked us out at Lae and Wau and finally, another debacle. The two day assault on our Hollandia Airfield complex drove us out of New Guinea proper. When Biak fell in early '44 we basically abandoned Rabaul and fell back to the Philippines. By summer the great base at Truk had become insignificant.

Phase 3, the Philippines, was to be the next big battle ground. When it started I had high hopes. We had deep resources there. 600,000 troops, hundreds of air bases, roughly 3,000 aircraft and no shortage of supplies. At the

start of the battle on 7 October 1944 we had air superiority in
that theater. For the first time since late '42 we owned the air
over the battlefield. The *Sword* was back in the game. That's
what I saw as a fighter pilot. Little did I know then that in a
few short weeks I would go from strategic fighter defense, to
tactical fighter defense, as the changing dynamics of reality
ushered in the radical new assault tactic...Kamikaze Warfare.
It promised to be a huge battle...and it was.

By the fall of '44 the heart of the struggle was centered on
the eastern Philippines. The Yanks came ashore at Leyte in
early October, by November my personal involvement in the
war changed emphasis. I remained loyal to Japan as did my
many brave friends and peers. But, above all, I fought to stay
alive now until the calamity was over. It was clear to all, we
could fore stall defeat but, we could not stop it.

I rose to the air with all the skill I could apply and faithfully fought off the ever increasing swarms of Hellcats and P-
38's as well as bomb runs by the many variations America employed. I continued to knock them down, always with an eye
to surviving. The Americans just the opposite had become
even bolder. They were confident, many experienced, some
even cocky with their prowess. They came in sweeps now, circling our aerodromes and taunting us to join combat. Many
stayed put on the ground the best of us rose to the contest. So
it went, day in and day out until, by around the end of December there were but a handful of our aircraft left in the islands.
By early '45 we had moved what was left to the next line of
defense, Phase 3, like Phase 1 and 2, had ended once again
in defeat. After I read this I thought about it for quite a while.
This is the synopsis of a then 31 year old very experienced
fighter pilot. He was not a man of command decision but, he
had fought all over the territory against the very best America and her Allies had to offer. He must have known even before his time out for injuries in late '43 that the outcome did
not look good. Yet, once healed he rejoined the effort in the

spring of '44 with everything he had to offer. Because of his experience he even compliments the enemy on their improved tactics and takes time to analyze the superior performance of the hot new P-38 fighter. He even knew about Americas number one Ace. It looks to me like he had a clear vision of where it was all going as early as spring 1944. Although almost momentarily optimistic in Oct of 1944 he must have been soon crestfallen at the weight of the enemy onslaught. Through it all he stayed to the battle, he rode it out to its ugly conclusion. He was an admirable man, I am so happy he survived. That was my Uncle, 1942 New Guinea to fall 1944 and the Battle of the Philippines.

Floyd Fulkerson in Basic Flight School as a trainee, 1942.

Wingman to The Aces

It wasn't long after I had met the old pilot that I came to the stream to see how he was doing that day. It was another clear sky day but, it was early June thus it was a little nippy. It turned out the old man had enough of the chill and was just getting ready to pack it in when I arrived. I helped him load his gear in the trunk and when finished he said almost absentmindedly, "hold on a second I've got something for you to read." Pulling a sheaf of papers from the glove box he then handed them to me. "Because it is such a long story I typed this up for you over the weekend." "This is Floyd Fulkerson's story son. He may have been the best wing man ever as you will soon discover". "I heard him speak of these things many times and finally I just put the story together". In addition he is involved in many engagements etc. that I will be telling you about.

At that point I received the papers and we parted. Later after supper I retired to my room and read it through. This is how the story goes.

I have known Floyd Fulkerson for decades. During that time period we have spent many hours discussing his personal involvement in WWII. As you will soon discover Floyd's personal story parallels those of some great historical fliers of the SWPA. The following is a factual account of his contribution to those historic events. Sometimes in his own words, sometimes in shared phrasing the following is the never before documented story of Lt. Floyd Fulkerson wingman to our nations greatest ever fighter pilots.

Hello, I'm Floyd Fulkerson. I was born and raised in Little Rock, Ar. 90 years later I'm still living near there in the little town of Scott just to the East in a set back on the bank of the Arkansas River. At age 21 I had completed my flying instruction as well as training into the Mitchell bomber. This is my story and it begins with my arrival June 1943 in the South West Pacific Area theater as a trained, combat ready, B-25 Mitchell Bomber pilot. In that capacity and flying out of the New Guinea, Port Moresby airfield complex I did several theater missions including one low level strafing run on the Japanese airfields at Rabaul. Especially, in those days, early in the war, this was an extremely risky endeavor.

One day, not long after arriving at that assignment and quite by chance I ran into an old college classmate in a Base Ops building while visiting a nearby base. This man, Alec Guerrey was in an administrative position of authority with the newly forming P-38 fighter deployment in that area. After exchanging hello's and some catching up on old times I let it be known that as much as I loved strafing the enemy with the Mitchell I would rather be dicing it up with a '38. Alec took to the suggestion and from his very special position set about pushing the buttons to make my dream a reality.

In another time and place the prospect of making this happen would have been bureaucratically nil. However, in the fast moving dynamics of front line warfare and with the distance from Command Headquarters scrutiny Alec somehow by subterfuge, bribery, or maybe magic never accounted for or explained managed to slip Floyd Fulkerson bomber pilot over to Floyd Fulkerson P-38 fighter pilot. In addition to the sleight of hand this required six weeks of cross training into the new operational discipline plus gunnery schooling as a fighter pilot. This was in the fall of 1943 and this changed status coincided with Gen Kenney's formation of the 475TH Fighter Group. This was to be Gen Kenney's pet outfit of mostly hand picked personnel and equipment wise it was to be built around the special capabilities of the newly introduced and almost revolutionary Lockheed P-38 Lightning fighter plane. By June of 1943 this newly formed unit was organized, trained to synch and deployed at the forward contact bases around Port Moresby.

In January 1944 I was assigned to the 431ST Fighter Squadron. Operating out of Dobodura, at age 22, I began my career as a combat fighter pilot. Starting then and with only an occasional ten day rest and recuperation break to Australia I would fly combat missions for one continuous year without break ranging as far away as Ceram, Indonesia, all over the New Guinea countryside plus surrounding waters and ultimately to the big shootout in the Philippines. From the beginning I flew the newly arriving "J" series Lightning and I served my entire tour of duty as a member of the 431ST squadron. This is significant in itself as the 431ST was the first to be equipped with the P-38 and it would be the only unit in the war to fly that single aircraft continuously until wars end. In addition, this unit would produce a multitude of top Aces including two of the very best. The 431ST along with the other squadrons the 432ND and 433RD went on to exceed Gen Kenney's expectations by a wide margin.

In the world of air combat there are "Great Aces" and "Great Wingmen" but, there are no "Great Aces" without "Great Wingmen". Floyd almost became an Ace ending the war with four confirmed kills of his own. But, more than that Floyd was a great wingman and in that role he flew with the greatest...protecting them, covering them and befriending them. Along with many other notables Floyd flew combat with Major Bong, Major McGuire, and even the much celebrated "Lone Eagle" Charles Lindbergh during his time spent with the 475TH Fighter Group. Whenever a celebrity or military luminary came to fly with the squadron Floyd was often picked to escort them because he was an excellent flyer, because he was reliable under fire, and he could be depended upon to cover the flight. Cover the shooter, that's what wingmen do. They protect the man that is on target from surprise attack. In this role he accompanied many of our great aces to achieve their successes. In particular he played an historic role in flying wing on Major Bong's last four kills starting 7 Dec 44 over Ormoc Bay, Philippines while flying cover for the Leyte invasion. On this occasion he was also in the company of number two Ace Major Thomas McGuire and Major Jack Rittmayer an old flying mate from Headquarters.

Altogether they were "Daddy Green Flight" orbiting the landing beach area at about 4,000 feet and about 16:00. Shortly after arriving on station Major Bong spotted and dispatched a Sally Bomber attempting to bomb the landing area. With Floyd as witness it became kill number 37. Let's let Floyd describe it in his own words.

"Suddenly Major Bong rolled out of formation and began a descent. As I watched his progress forward I began to perceive his quarry low off the water in the distance. A Betty bomber was lining up for a run on our troops in the assault landing area. This break with flight discipline momentarily angered me. As wingman my job was to cover him during our mission. Combat procedure required him to call out the target location and then to initiate his attack. Don't get me wrong I have great respect for Major Bong. He was a very important part of the war effort and I did not want anything to happen to him on my watch. Suppressing my anger I took a quick look around the whole area and breathed a little easier. There were no more enemy aircraft in site. Just the same I rolled off and headed in his direction just to make sure. As I approached a little higher and just behind he was beginning the attack on the Betty. From my vantage point I could see it all quite clearly. Richard was a good fighter driver but, his forte was gunnery. Peering down from this position I watched a master do his deadly work. Approaching about a hundred fifty yards from the rear and a little high to the bomber he snapped off a quick burst and the tail gunner got chewed out along with shards of metal and Plexiglas. Free of the tail gunner threat he rose up a little more, closed to about 50 yards and with about 3 degrees of cant to the left began to work the left engine area. I could see the hits sparkling, pieces coming away and in seconds smoke began to trail from the engine. I scanned the area again and as I looked back down he started rolling the nose of the '38 to the right. Methodically he stitched through the hull and cockpit area on his way to the right engine pod. It was almost surgical. His aim so precise hardly any of the tracers passed the target. A few seconds burst and the right engine began to disintegrate. Soon the Betty failed and fell off into the sea. In just a matter of moments it was over. It was a privilege to have flown with him and I treasure the memories but, just the same, later that day when we returned to base I gave him a piece of my mind. I even made note of the incident officially. Even though he outranked me...it's mentioned in the squadron history." But, that would come later in the day. Just as he rejoined us a flight of five low flying Tojos appeared and it was clear their intent was to ram troop transports gathered in the landing area. McGuire spotted their approach and ordered Daddy Green Flight to attack and destroy.

We all broke flight discipline at this point. It was rare but, there was an overriding imperative. The anchored troop transports were naked to the new innovation of Kamikaze attack. En masse, we ditched directives and charged ahead to meet the challenge.

While the others sought a target I latched onto one and followed it into heavy anti-aircraft fire emanating from the fleet vessels trying to ward off attack. Yea, it's risky business flying into fleet anti-aircraft fire but, I had a great fighter and a job to do. So, I ignored the threat and drove my Lightning right up to within about 50 feet of him and set that 50 cal buzz saw to work. "I wanted to get right on his ass to make damn sure I knocked him down before he hit a troop transport". I succeeded and the Tojo exploded in a fireball and a shower of parts approximately twenty feet off the water erupting with such violence that the water beneath foamed from the splashing parts. Having no choice I hung on and flew through the fireball and debris. Thinking at the time to myself. "This is it ...I'm done".

Seconds later Floyd found himself safe and still flying at wave height. Pulling back hard on the stick he zoomed back to 3,000 feet where the flight gathered and headed back to home base at Dulag Airfield. In the melee he witnessed Major Bong's second kill, another of the flight of five Tojos. McGuire and Rittmayer each bagged one of them rounding out what was considered a good effort by all. Once landed and safely tucked into a parking point Floyd and several ground crewmen made a special inspection of the aircraft fully expecting to find damage after the hair raising encounter. To their collective astonishment there was no evidence of damage nor flame scorching from the close proximity to the exploding Tojo.

On the 15TH of Dec on a sweep over Panubulon Is Major Bong bagged another Oscar while I accompanied him in the wingman function. Covering his back I watched as he hit it with a couple of bursts. Soon, pieces coming away, it began to head down and I watched as it crashed into the ocean and exploded. This was number 39 for Bong and I officially verified the kill on our return to base. However, before returning to home base we flew back over Negros Island where I made a high speed low level strafing pass on Tanzan Airdrome. Out of the approximately 20 enemy aircraft sighted on Tanzan I destroyed two Jacks and an Oscar all three in a row in the process of taking off. In addition I nailed two Oscars at rest near the far end of the runway. It was the fastest I had ever flown a P-38 close to the ground. I went in at 410 MPH well aware that Jap ack ack was very accurate. Even at that speed they very nearly got me blowing my canopy off half way through the run. Bong hovered at altitude as he had been restricted from strafing and to cover me on my effort. Coming off the run I chandelled up to Bongs altitude, assumed the wingman position and we returned uneventfully to Dulag.

Floyd was lucky indeed to survive this very close call. The Japanese were very good at anti-aircraft defense and final after war analysis determined that roughly 40 percent of our "Shot Down" losses were attributed to ground fire mostly during low level attacks.

Two days later on the 17TH of Dec Bong and I were at it again. I had the great privilege of covering this great Ace on what would become a history making sweep over the landing beach on Mindoro Island. At 4:25PM and at about 9,000 feet Major Bong closed on an Oscar and as I explained it in the confirming action report filed back at Dulag. "I saw Dick close in on the Oscar from dead astern and fire a short burst which brought pieces from the Oscar. The Oscar turned right and with another burst from Maj. Bong, did a half roll, trailing fire and crashed into the jungle." This was the 40TH confirmed kill for Major Bong making him America's "Ace of Aces," probably for all time.

Once again Lt. Fulkerson had done the wingman's job. On this occasion sharing in and ensuring success in this historic career crowning achievement. As documented, Floyd flew protection and confirmation on all four of Bong's final victories. Of the four members of the historic Daddy Green Flight to include McGuire and Rittmayer Lt. Fulkerson would ultimately be the only one to survive the war. For Major Bong the war was over as he was grounded by Gen. Kenney and returned to the states arriving in San Francisco in time for New Year celebrations and an adoring public reception.

For Floyd Fulkerson the war continued and on 20 Dec he touched another piece of history, although the significance was unknown to him at the time. On that date flight records indicate he started a combat mission in aircraft serial number 44-23296. This is one of those "Happy Stories" that occasionally happen even in war time. As it turned out this particular aircraft was the 5,000[TH] Lockheed Lightning produced and being very proud of that contribution Lockheed painted it a brilliant vermillion red, named it *YIPPEE* and sent it on tour around the country to push war bonds and Lockheed Corp. The appearance of this aircraft caused a sensation at air shows around the country and it soon became a widely photographed icon of the war time period. In time the P.R. touring ended and the aircraft returned to the Burbank plant where it was stripped and returned to battle dress.   Overseas the war was still raging, combat aircraft attrition was high, and subsequently *YIPPEE* was loaded up and sent to the Philippines to aid in that effort.

As it turned out this aircraft was assigned to the 431ST Fighter Squadron at Dulag, the unit Floyd flew with as a part of the 475TH Fighter Group. The aircraft somehow arrived without fanfare and on this day Floyd flew it into battle as his normal mount was temporarily out of service. Alas, records indicate an early return to base from some unexplained problem and before the aircraft could be repaired and returned to duty it got caught up in a ground crash event and was so heavily damaged it had to be salvaged. A pleasant, light, historical note to share but, the cold realities of war marched on as within days the life and death nature of the struggle would resume.

Five days later on Christmas day 1944 Lt. Floyd Fulkerson flew his 125TH and final combat mission. It was a big battle. The target was the huge flight complex at Clark airfield as well as the many surrounding airfields in the Manila area. Heavy bombers were brought in to savage the airfields and all the fighters that could be mustered were thrown into the event. An excited Lt. Fulkerson climbed into his trusty old mount emblazoned with the moniker *Who's Next..?* on the nose and flew toward the target zone. The Japanese were incensed by the affront and threw approximately 70 fighters into the melee. When the battle unfolded it quickly turned into a free for all. It was a fighter pilots dream and Floyd very quickly tailed and shot down two Jack fighters in quick succession.

Again, let's let him explain it in his own words. "I homed in on a pair of Jacks making a run on a box of B-24's. Rising to the rear of the second one back I hit him with a 25 degree deflection shot and he spun off toward the jungle and burst on impact. Immediately I kicked in a little left rudder, lined up the leader and started chewing on him with the 50's. Taking hits he started a shallow turn to the right and I pulled tighter raking the flank through the wing root and cockpit area. As chunks flew out he rolled left and headed down trailing smoke. Moments later I watched him crash into the jungle below and explode."

One more and Floyd would officially join the society of Aces. With the war mission paramount and his personal goals in mind he bore in on his third target of the fight and in the process he violated one of the most fundamental rules of aerial combat. In his excitement and ambition he ran off and left his wingman. Better still, once again lets hear how it went in his own words.

Looking around for more action I found number three crossing right to left in front of me and just about the same altitude. I kicked the big twin fan to the left, and just as I lined him up I noticed tracers passing to my right and I started taking hits in the tail. I could hear the shells hitting and I could feel the aircraft shudder. Those booms taking hits were like a tuning fork sending me the news. Quickly I nosed over full throttle and dove off to escape. I soon outdistanced them and they turned back to the fight. Once free I looked around for my wingman who was nowhere to be seen. As I maneuvered and glanced around I thought I could see spray trailing from the tail area. Very soon my worst fears were realized. They had perforated my radiators located in the booms. Both engines were heating up rapidly. The good news, my airplane was flying just fine. The bad news. I was a long way from home and it was plain to see ...*Who's Next..?* wasn't going to carry me back home to safety. As the temp needles headed toward the pegs I located what looked like a suitable place to set her down so I banked and headed that way. Hopefully I had found a place where the Japanese wouldn't be down there to greet me. Only time would tell. Right now I had to get her down and fast. The landing site turned out to be a rice paddy about 50 miles North of Manila and near the town of Santa Maria.

Flaring and slowing he brought the big fighter down in the paddy in a controlled manner but, took a nasty lick at the far side of the field when it encountered a built up containment berm. The heavy jolt came at the end of its slide however, with enough of an impact to crack two of Floyd's vertebrae. As he wiggled from the wreckage the remains burst into flames ultimately destroying the aircraft. Lucky for him Philippino guerrillas had witnessed his plight, rushed to his aid, and spirited him away to the mountainous jungle surround before the Japanese could capture him.

The next five weeks were spent evading the Japanese as a guest of the guerrillas who quickly passed word back to US authorities that he was at least alive and well. For most people their story would go something like: rescue, out of action due to injury. Needing long recovery, return to states, end of war, end of story. Not so with the remarkable Floyd Fulkerson. Rather like an attendant in the court of a monarch Floyd somehow was always close to and a part of the action. Once again he moved with the center of gravity and soon became a party to the rambling ground battle. That's why he was chosen so often to fly wing. He served with discipline and when given the opportunity executed with precision. His career was not celebrity stellar although he very nearly became an Ace. More important Floyd was an enabler. He was the kind of guy whose efforts helped others to become great. He was the ultimate wingman. In that role he served to support top shooters over thousands of miles and as he wryly described it: *124 ½ missions.* He flew with them, guarding them, into the mouth of the dragon. The great names I've already mentioned, his most intense moments already defined. There is still even more to Floyd than this. Beginning with his rescue by guerrillas he resolved to continue his resistance on the ground until he could be rescued. After an initial three weeks of healing and with communication provided again by the guerillas he linked up with two OSS agents. One from Laramie, Wyoming and one from Pennsylvania. One night in mid January 1945 along with these two men he participated in a late night commando mission deep behind enemy lines North of Manila.

Together, the three of them slipped behind Japanese lines in a successful effort to destroy a rail road bridge crucial to the Japanese defense posture in that area. Braving certain torture and probably death if captured they successfully dropped the span late at night with dynamite and then faded away without discovery to an area of safety. For this heroic ground activity Lt. Fulkerson Army Aviator was awarded a Bronze Combat Star by the US Army.

Later in the month with the aid of a water buffalo borrowed from a farmer he cleared a landing strip in the jungle from which he was eventually plucked by a small Army L-5 observation plane just barely able to clear the tree tops during takeoff. To have come in contact with clandestine agents was remarkable in itself. To participate with them on a combat mission and arrange his own escape by constructing "Fulkerson Airfield" was like something out of the fictional comic strip *Terry and the Pirates.* With his self arranged rescue his war ended as it would be concluded before his damaged back healed. For Lt. Fulkerson it was time to rest and deservedly so. He had served first his nation and then his fellow flyers admirably. Eventually after the war ended and there was time to address things left undone Lt. Fulkerson was awarded a Silver Star by the United States Navy for his action braving fleet anti-aircraft fire and saving naval personnel from Japanese Kamikaze attack at Ormoc Bay 7 Dec 1944. As far as is known this is the only instance of an Army Air Force member receiving a Silver Star from the US Navy. This now concludes the story of the contribution of Lt. Floyd Fulkerson 431ST Squadron fighter pilot of the 475Th Fighter Group 5Th Air Force from Jan 1944 to Jan 1945.

On a final note I asked Floyd about his thoughts on some of his fellow flyers performance in combat, flying in general, and personality traits. The following are his selective comments on some of them.

Major Richard Bong: Not as good a performance flyer as the best but, a fearless fighter pilot and the "The best shooter he ever flew with, his marksmanship was phenomenal."

Major Thomas McGuire: An excellent squadron commander as he was even handed and careful to be fair and treated everyone equally. Confident leadership in battle and the best flyer he ever flew with and that he enjoyed flying missions with him because he was so good. Also, "One helluva poker player," "The Lone Eagle," "Charles Lindbergh," a "Prince of a Guy." Cordial, sophisticated. Knew more about airplanes than anyone he ever met. Freely shared his knowledge to improve their flying and showed them how to extend the range of their fighters to give threat dimension not until then realized. He came into the presence of men in their early twenties as a middle aged legend but, did not wear his fame on his sleeve. "I felt comfortable in his presence and enjoyed talking to him."

What happened to Tommy McGuire? In my opinion: "Knowing him personally, having flown with him personally, knowing how ambitious he was, knowing how superbly he could handle a P-38, knowing how badly he yearned to become Ace of Aces. Again, in my opinion, in his eagerness and self assuredness...I believe he simply reached too far."

When asked if the guns would shake the Plane and be heard when used he went into detail. Pointing out their 3-4 foot proximity to the cockpit he said. "Yes, they were very loud, they shook the plane and that the cockpit quickly filled with smoke". He then smiled, and his eyes lit up as he explained further. "I loved the smell of gun smoke in the cockpit."

One final observation has echoed back to me from the time Floyd brought it up on our very first visit. It was brought on in open general conversation about war and it's effect on people and how did they respond to the stress and fear and excitement and all the many emotional things that go on in these circumstances. He then remarked in a poignant and serious statement: "You could see in a fellow pilots eyes when he had *given up* or lost his edge or fire for the contest." Soon after: "That they would be lost...almost," he said, "as if they had surrendered to an inevitability."

I think it is an important impression from a man who lived the event. I think it is important to include it in the historical record.

These then are the remembrances of a man still living. Remembrances from a three dimensional airscape six decades in the past. Even though Floyd is now 90 years old his memories of these men and these events are sharp and easily recalled. Bong and McGuire are still 24 years old and he sees them in their prime. No one can ever reach out and touch them again. Neither can Floyd but, he can see them as yesterday...hear their voices excited in combat or over beers at the Dobo "Club 38." He can hear those Allisons firing off at dawn...smell the cordite in the cockpit...close his eyes and fly through an exploding airplane. This he can do as we never can. He has taken the time to impart these experiences as best he can for our benefit. We are so very, fortunate he gives

us these accounts. Very soon there will be no more fighter pilots. Technology is obsoleting them rapidly. This was their
apex in the century long tenure of manned aerial combat. You
have now heard the story of a man who lived and fought at the
spear point of the battle. Thank you sir so very, very much for
sharing your story.

Well when I finished that I was glad he had given me the information typed out rather than orally. This man had packed
a life time of excitement and high risk into one year. All before the age of 24. As I drifted into sleep I had to wonder if we
today have what it takes to equal their performance.

Bong's Last Combat Mission

On a day trip across northern Wisconsin the old pilot told me of Bong's last mission and the related conversations recounted here. When I returned home that evening I jotted down the fundamentals and in the next few days I researched the time line and read all the published descriptions I could find. When I felt confident of the facts I did my best to reconstruct the activities as if he were retelling it himself. Thus it begins.

At 1450 hours on the afternoon of 17 Dec 1944 Daddy Special Flight lifted into the air at Dulag AB, the Philippines. They were bound for the Mindoro Island combat zone to the west. Their mission, protect the beach head landing area and intercept enemy aircraft. At a casual glance this formation would have looked like any other two element flight off on a routine combat patrol. Not so, this quartet consisted of Major Bong, Major McGuire, Major Rittmayer and Lt Fulkerson. This was no ordinary combat mission. Make no mistake about it, plain and simple, this gathering was on a hunting trip. At this moment in time between the four of them they had over 2,000 hours cumulative combat experience and 75 confirmed kills ranging from a high of 39 to 2. They averaged two and one half years in theater and had flown in and over every major contested area of the SWPA often together. This was the A Team, Satan's Angels of the 475TH Fighter Group. Before the mission ended at 1830 hours Major Bong would bag his fortieth kill and with that the title "Ace of Aces" probably for all time. As we shall see, there was a lot at stake for everyone involved.

First let's review them individually. We'll start with Rittmayer and McGuire. These two had been flying together as far back as the Aleutians in '42. Jack was a natural staff man. He was already gaining traction at 5TH Air force Headquarters. He was on loan from HQ to fly as a guest with the 431ST Fighter Squadron. Interestingly he had attended Annapolis before migrating to the Army AF. Jack was likeable, he was ambitious and he intended to career up after the war. He had three kills when he took off and he wanted very much to hit five and the vaunted Ace status that would accelerate his career prospects. It would be a rewarding day for Jack. When the sun set that day he would be one mark away from the prize.

Major McGuire had flown with the 431ST Squadron from the beginning. He eventually became the Sq Commander and he made it the best in the Group. He had recently relinquished command and assumed a Group staff position. This arrangement provided by Gen Kenney gave him the freedom like Bong to pick his flights and areas to compete. Basically he still flew as a 431ST Sq member. With thirty one kills he trailed Bong by eight. However, he knew once Bong hit forty he would be sent stateside leaving himself the opportunity to overtake his record. Highly competitive he would do his best to gain even one kill on Bong if he could. Today he would come up short. While Bong and Rittmayer scored Tommie would have to forfeit his attack option and fulfill his responsibility to provide cover.

Lt Fulkerson flying wing to McGuire had his own ambition to pursue. Like Major Rittmayer he was also scrambling to attain Ace status. On this day with two kills he likely felt more pressure than the rest to find a target. Now in mid Dec they were all aware, with fewer targets, they were running out of war. Every opportunity could be their last. Still, foremost in his mind was the awareness to stay alert, he was nearing the end of his tour in theater and he had every intention of returning home. I've already referenced the steady, reliable wing-man capability Floyd demonstrated over time and in excess of one hundred missions. Once again he would fill that role when, caught up in a breach of combat discipline he quickly altered the battle dynamic to assure the attack success of Major Bong and with determination flew tight with him to make sure nothing happened to him on his watch. In doing so he would bear witness to an historic moment and forever enjoin himself and his role to that achievement.

Last there is Major Bong. In some ways it was easier for him than the rest. Reason would suggest it was just a matter of time. He, like Tommie, was free to roam at will. Wherever the daily intelligence pointed to better odds he could make the adjustment to the most likely scenario. For the last few weeks he had chosen to fly with the 431ST Sq. He was amongst old friends, flying out of Dulag they were in the thick of the fight. Lastly, he knew he could depend on the experienced men accompanying him. Much was at stake on his next kill. This would be it, number forty. The magic number might as well have been glowing in his sight ring. All he had to do was be careful, be thorough, and within a few days he would be successful. On his two trips back to the states he had tasted celebrity and adulation. One more victory and his future was secured.

The 431ST was the leading combat Sq in the Pacific. Just eight days later they would be the first squadron to pass two hundred kills. A feat they accomplished in just seventeen months. Ten days earlier these four men had destroyed five enemy aircraft in just a few minutes of furious combat. Satan's Angels were a formidable weapon Dick was happy to work with. This then was the quartet headed for the landing zone. They were experienced, they were confident and they were on the prowl.

About an hour later just as they were closing on the Mindoro beach at 9,000 feet Maj. Bong spotted two Oscars a bit above them heading north. Immediately the engagement began to unfold. This is how it was explained to me by Lt Fulkerson.

In the pre flight briefing session earlier it had been determined that as ranking officer Major Bong would lead the flight on today's mission. He placed Major Rittmayer as his wing man in the lead element followed by the trailing element with Lt Fulkerson flying wing to Major McGuire. Along with this formation he briefly discussed anticipated weather en route as well as in the Mindoro patrol area. In addition to the usual reminder to remain alert he ended the briefing with this final emphasis here described as closely as possible. "If we spot the enemy await my command. I will issue the orders for attack. It is likely I will split the lead element if the situation warrants. If so, the trailing element will divide, McGuire to Rittmayer, Fulkerson follow me". This is a close repetition of the actual conversation in the pre flight meeting as told to me by Lt Fulkerson. It was an important departure from protocol and deserves mention as a matter of clarification to the historical record.

Even though this was a violation of combat procedure there was no questioning Bong and there was no further discussion of his decision. One can only speculate on his motives. As previously covered Richard Bong was near the end of a long and stressful combat career. Even though he had R and R breaks he was surely at a point where he wanted it to end. Above all he wanted it to end smoothly and safely. It was thus his show and it would be done per his wishes. Dick was known to help other pilots in their aspirations as well as often giving kills to other pilots along the way. Maybe he wanted to help Jack step into the future by sharing the targets.

What he did know with certainty. The two guys flying 2ND element were the best 5TH Air Force had to cover the engagement. Split the targets with Jack, ensure the enemy attrition, count coup and go home. In addition, this arrangement kept a hungry McGuire out of the contest at least at the beginning of the fight while assuring Floyd would be there to cover him if he got jumped.

"With this as the back ground Major Bong turned the flight to the chase while ascending a bit higher for the advantage. It took about 10 minutes to position on the Japanese who maintained their course until the attack began. As we approached the duo Major Bong led with Major Rittmayer flying his wing. Trailing a little higher and to the right Major McGuire with myself positioned as his wingman. As we initiated the attack the Japanese split, with one descending and turning right while the other ascended as he banked left. It is likely, with their agility, they hoped to circle back on us. It was not to be. Major Bong led us well. When they split, Major Bong the flight leader, ordered Major Rittmayer to pursue the Oscar breaking left while he closed to the one breaking right. In a few seconds both aircraft were down, that action has been covered in a prior discussion." This was a clear breach of regulation combat procedure and attack protocol. This splitting of the lead element required the second element in turn to violate procedure by splitting to cover them. A lot can be made of this or nothing can be made of it. After all it was a successful attack on the enemy. Major Bong got his historic mark and everyone arrived back at Dulag safe and sound. Initially this lapse in procedure went without notice. A few days later Major Bong left the theater and the war forever. Just eight days later moments after his second kill of the day Floyd Fulkerson would be shot down over Manila. Fourteen days later Major McGuire and Major Rittmayer both perished on the same mission. Although Floyd survived that event an injury incurred on crash landing effectively ended his participation in the air war and he was soon sent home. Nine months later Dick Bong perished in an accidental crash just as the door was closing on the war.

Thus Floyd became the only surviving member of this historical engagement. Like millions of others, when the war ended he returned to a long and successful civilian career. In time people who make it their business to study these things began to sift through information. At some point it was noticed that this engagement had violated command procedure. Also the similar event at Ormoc Bay 7 Dec began to be referenced. In the 17 Dec engagement it became a question. Did Major Bong order the split in the lead element or did Major Rittmayer cut to the attack to satisfy his own ambition? For the record, you now know exactly how the event transpired. There is still more to the story and this is how it unfolded back at Dulag.

Again, as related to me by Lt Fulkerson, as you may recall. Major Bong had also ignored procedure 10 days earlier when breaking away for an attack on a Sally bomber. That incident had riled Floyd enough that his account of his displeasure was recorded in the daily unit history. We have to keep in mind here the difference in rank. A 1ST Lt has to be very careful to challenge a major over official policy. That did not stop Floyd from chiding Bong back at the barracks when he famously said to him. "It's a good thing you didn't shoot down three today as you couldn't handle three victory rolls." Thus, needling Bong this way he expressed his displeasure with Dick in a manner that would not promote an official reprimand.

The sequel to this would occur after the famous 17 Dec fortieth kill flight. Everyone did their normal after flight debriefing and then returned to their tents. Including Floyd Fulkerson, who added this interesting anecdote. While lying on his cot resting an hour or so after clearing debriefing Floyd was approached by Major Bong for assurance that Floyd had confirmed his recent kill. The exact conversation clearly remembered many years later as follows. "Well Lt, did you see the plane I shot down?" To which Floyd replied.

"What plane?" Brushing that off Bong inquired the same a second time to which Floyd replied. "Maybe I did...and maybe I didn't". Bong thinking this to somehow be a joke inquired in kind again. The same answer followed. Not getting the anticipated results a now somewhat agitated Bong turned and left the tent in a huff.

Keep in mind these were young men, barely past their teens. They were hot young fighter pilots. They had big egos and big ambition, surely some envy and maybe some jealousy too. Bong was the best that was self evident. Maybe they expected more out of him than themselves including observing discipline. There may have been a rank differential that precluded a reprimand for violating discipline twice in 10 days but, Floyd had Dick on a skewer and he let him roast for about an hour. Finally, Floyd acquiesced and acknowledged that, yes, he Floyd Fulkerson, had witnessed and confirmed Bongs crowning fortieth kill. Indeed, that he had done this immediately after landing. With that Major Bong thanked him, noted that it had been a pleasure flying together and went about his business. A few days later a grounded Major Bong shipped out for the states and Floyd never saw him again.

For the record, this is how these events were related to me by Floyd Fulkerson many years later on an occasion when we were reminiscing about the war. With that the conversation changed over to interesting sites along the highway, how great the smoked trout salad was at the restaurant in Bayfield and soon we were back in Poplar where he dropped me at my place.

So, we finally have the answer to the questions surrounding the mission on 17 Dec. I found through further research that this was a common topic among historians and buffs of the era. Indeed Bong's brother Carl addressed the question in his excellent book "Dear Mom So We Have A War". He discusses this question in detail on page 466. This following the very brief actual combat report by Dick reprinted on page 465 that omitted any mention of the pre flight instructions or his ordering Rittmayer to attack the splitting and ascending Oscar thus compromising the safety of the entire element. As for me putting all this together with my brief knowledge left me impressed but exhausted so I reached over, shut the light off and drifted to sleep chasing Oscars over Mindoro.

Five Card Studs...the Click of the Chips

Here we were again at the fishing hole he in the shadow of the pines and I next to the birch stand to the west side of the trail. It was late afternoon on a beautiful, sunny summer day. About 70 degrees with a now and then waft of breeze. We had been sitting here quietly for maybe 15 to 20 minutes. The old man was using live bait and a bobber today, pan fishing more or less and he was close to having supper caught. Some nice crappie, a couple of blue gill and one bull head. When I arrived a half hour ago he had remarked that a twin to the bull head would round out a nice meal for him and his wife.

There was a healthy stand of wild grass to the right of his chair and he was chewing on a long piece when I arrived. This is a Wisconsin thing, everyone seemed to do it. They don't do this in the big city where I'm from although I remember the same grass growing in parks and other places like the river banks. I had come to enjoy it myself. So, I walked over and snapped a piece off. It was about 15 inches long and about 3/8 inch in diameter. Being late summer the tassel was a rich whitish green and heavy as the seeds still clung. You can't describe the taste. The stems are ripe with water and the texture is crunchy. It is overall a pleasant experience and maybe explains why so many indulge and cows love it too.

With me seated again we both chomped away and casually followed the endless, ever changing pattern of eddies, swirls and ripples as the stream slid by. The water is clear and where it is placid you can see the moss on the rocks beneath along with pebbly or sometimes sandy areas. The old man had positioned the bait and bobber about 8 feet from the bank and maybe 2 feet deep. He was using a light rod and reel with a two inch minnow hooked behind the dorsal fin. It was a non vital area and the minnow would occasionally jiggle the bobber as he moved about.

It had been quite a while since the last catch and the old pilot suggested off handedly as he checked the condition of the bait that he might have caught everything hanging out in the pool. As he said that I thought I saw a shadow moving through the rippled area. I just wasn't sure. Between tree shadows and bright sunlight the eyes played tricks. As I continued to gaze I let my eyes rove in an ever greater circle from the rapids to the calm area of the pool. I did not see anything further beneath the water and gave it up as an imaginary sighting.

After a bit I kind of fell into a trance enjoying the tranquility of it all and daydreaming about the big city I would soon be returning to. Suddenly, from the corner of my eye I noticed the bobber livening up. Right about then I saw a fin break the ripples and as it turned perpendicular to the current it vanished beneath the surface. A couple of seconds later the bobber went down and I could see it about a foot under the water and heading for the far side of the pool. Just then the old man gave a backward heave over his shoulder with the rod to set the hook and with that the battle was on.

With the line tight the fish made two quick circles of the pool then headed straight for the rough water area. The old man on his feet now was having none of that. With bent rod he kept hauling back while spinning the reel take up as fast as he could. Short of the rocks the fish rolled up to the left just breaking an inch of his back clear of the water and with a wet fan spray he snapped around and headed straight toward the old man at the waters edge. A lot was happening real fast in a relatively small area. The old pilot was good. I could see him grimace as he reeled furiously to keep the line tight. The grass stem had fallen from his mouth and he was red faced with the effort but, he was winning. The fish was trying hard to get loose. Moving probably as fast as he could he came out of the water at about a thirty degree angle and shook himself violently. I can still see it now. Back and forth, head and tail, bowing from side to side, jaws snapping as the line chaffed at the corners of his mouth. Now fully exposed I marveled at his size and coloring which was striking. He had a dark back, mottled flanks and a silver belly with a long snout in front of flared, blood red gills. The old man was right on top of this guy and when the fish broke water he swung the rod hard to the left and flipped the prize onto the grassy river bank. I then jumped up and after running over to the wildly flopping fish I grabbed the line just above the leader and tugged upward while placing my foot on his flank to still him.

This was a big fish. He was well over two feet long and he had a lot of teeth that he was trying to sink into something. I kept the pressure between the line and my foot as the old man ran a needle nose pliers down the leader to the hook. Very carefully he worked the hook loose from back near the gill. This guy got lucky he had not fully swallowed the hook when it was set. The fish didn't seem appreciative as he kept thrashing and I was certain trying hard to bite me. I think I must have looked scared for the old man chuckled as he directed me to return the fish to the water. I did as I was instructed and as I bent to the stream edge it was clear there would be no oxygenation release. Sensing freedom the fish began to squirm vigorously and soon dropped from my hands to the water. With contact he spanked the water hard with his tail and headed to center stream like a bullet.

I must have looked a little nonplussed for when I turned around the old pilot was laughing. "Okay," I said. "What's going on here? Why are we not keeping this fish?" he then replied. "That son was your first encounter with a Muskie,

Hopefully it won't be your last." He then sat down and began to bait the line for a new effort. Before I could speak again he said to me. "That was a juvenile son kind of like yourself a lot of energy with a lot of learning to do. That is the top fresh water predator. He was less than thirty one inches so, must be returned to the wild. That's the only reason I caught him. If he had been an adult he would have crossed the rapids or headed for a log to wrap the line up. They are very hard to catch once they mature. It takes them about three years to exceed thirty one inches at which time the DNR considers them fair game to keep."

"They are a very aggressive fish, you were lucky you were not bitten. When you fish them in open water you shoot the big ones with a .22 before boarding them just to be safe. The natives don't call them fresh water sharks for nothing. A big one can run 50 to 60 inches, take 45 minutes to land and take a finger or shred a hand. They will attack you in the water so don't even think about going skinny dipping." At that we broke into nervous laughter and I filed that info away into the scary memory bank. After this spell of excitement we collected ourselves and sat back down. The old pilot still wanted one more for his supper.

I went back to daydreaming touching at times on images he had already described to me when suddenly it occurred to me to ask what all these pilots did with their free time like when it was storming and they couldn't fly. There was a pause as he thought for a moment and then he replied. "Cards, we played cards and I wish you could have seen it. These were steel eyed fighter pilots and they played poker like the wild men of western lore. Tommie McGuire, Jack Rittmayer and Gerry Johnson all started flying combat together in the Aleutians back in early 42, and of course there is nothing to do there but play cards off duty. By the time they made it to Dobo they were sharks. Bong was another one. All you read about is his baby face and his angelic demeanor. Let me tell you, he was ruthless at poker. His main wingman Floyd Fulkerson was an accomplished player also. There were others equally as good. The games were spirited, sometimes tense but, nobody got angry or jealous. Well, not often anyway. The games went on island to island, base to base but, it really got cooking in the fall of '44. Once we got to Dulag most everybody had picked up some rank. We had flight pay we had combat pay, you know, we had money and no place to spend it.

So, when the rains set in the pots took off. I remember one particular episode this bored Lt Col showed up and joined in. He was an office type, didn't fly. There was no rank at the poker table still, this guy was pretty cocky. He was from back east somewhere. Anyway, after a bit he's popping off about bluffing with a strong suggestion he's the best there is. At some point Floyd Fulkerson says to the guy.'Do you know what checking the senses means?' The Col then replied. 'Of course I do.' But, he didn't, and Floyd a pretty good judge of real poker players correctly perceived that he didn't understand the reference. A little while later Fulkerson has him all set up in a draw down just the two of them. Floyd with some artful raising drives the guy to fold for a pretty big pot at least a couple hundred bucks. As he is scraping the money in Floyd shows his hand which, would have lost to the Col had he not fallen for the bluff. As he did this he said: 'Now you know what checking the senses means.' The Col then drew himself up in a huff and left, we all had a good laugh over that.

Well, anyway, we had some real rounders there in October and November. I know for a fact that Bong won a couple grand in a couple games and sent it home. Not long after that he turned around and lost about 1500. Then pretty soon he hit the forty kill mark and Gen Kenney sent him home for good. We never saw Gerry Johnson much anymore as he was running the 49TH Fighter Group up at Tacloban. He just didn't have time to spare like before. Too bad, he was real good at bluffing. That guy was fearless and he would do it to you with that big friendly grin of his. Next to Tommie he was the best fighter pilot I ever saw.

Right about then Tommie got a bad run of luck going. I know Floyd fronted him losses and loans, five grand over about six weeks. Floyd told me that himself. Those two got on real well. They were both from patrician backgrounds, good educations and all that. They didn't either one probably have to go to war. They could have pulled strings if they wanted like some did. But, they didn't, they volunteered. They were good people both of them, outstanding pilots, everybody liked them. Floyd's money went down with Tommie over Negros but, I think the loss of his friend meant much more to him.

It just went like that wild and wooly through about Christmas and then it was over. Some left, some were shot down. My time was up, I went home in December and I never saw most of them again. I heard Floyd survived the war okay. Of course I read about Tommie and Jack and later Bong gone too. Many years later I ran into Floyd at an event and we reminisced about a lot of things. I can still see them around that table, Laughing, grinning, bluffing. I can see them gesturing, see the chips being tossed in...I can hear the swish of the cards being dealt. All around the table...five card studs."

He paused then as he reflected back sort of caught in the moment. Everything changed then. His deportment, his speech lowered, his gaze fixed somehow far away. It was like that warm summer day on the beach earlier this summer. He wasn't fishing anymore he was back at the table with the guys. They were not Colonels and Majors and lieutenants. They were his friends, Richard, Jack and Tommie. Gerry and Floyd were there too. It was quite a moment to witness. The indelible camaraderie and intimacy of their time together was still with him after all these decades had passed.

He was quiet for a few moments and then as his consciousness returned to the river bank he said this. "You know between the hands and bluffs they used to talk about going fishing. Bong and Jack and Gerry Johnson were always talking about meeting up after the war to go fishing. Richard wanted them to come up and stay at the farm at Poplar and hunt and fish. If they had made it they would have fished the same places we do. I think about them every year when I come up here. I am so grateful I made it to here. It's a wonderful place to relax and remember."

The next bite never came. Once again it was getting late on the day. As the old pilot packed things up he said they could add some French fries and cole slaw to the fish he had and all together it would be enough to make a meal. Once again we parted, him in his Buick, me on my bike. Later that night as I lay in my bed I tried to imagine these guys around a poker table. I had seen all of their photos so I could visualize them gesturing, laughing, bluffing, under a blue smoke haze in the dim tent light. Fighter pilots at play...modern day gun slingers in an old west format.

As I slipped into slumber I was sure I could hear the click of the chips.

Reaching For The Brass Ring

Unless it was raining hard or excessively chilly the old man would come to the same spot on the bank and at least for a few hours he would try to catch something. Today it was misting with a dark heavy cloud cover threatening more. Sure enough as I made the turn and crossed the bridge I could see the top of his Buick just above the embankment that ran parallel to the parking lot. As I rode up he said "welcome" and motioned for me to have a seat.

We made some small talk and he remarked that the fish were not hungry today but, that maybe he didn't really care. We sat quietly for a while each lost in our own thoughts. I watched the eddies in the stream while he kept an eye on his line. After a bit he wound his line in, stripped the worm off the hook and fixed it to an eyelet half way down the rod and tightened the slack until the reel clicked.

He turned slightly in his chair to face me and said. "You've heard me speak of Tommie McGuire before son and you now know quite a bit about him. Today I'm going to talk to you about what happened to him on his last combat mission. First I was not there but, I've seen the mission reports and a lot has been written subsequent to this event, much of it based on the testimony of the three survivors of the engagement. Two Americans, one Japanese."

This then is what I can tell you about the last flight of Major McGuire. Like Major Bong, as a Group Operations Officer he now had the privilege of flying, when and where he chose. In addition, because of his rank and position, he had access to the latest intelligence reports on enemy position and strength. So, on the night of 6 Jan 45 the information he was scanning would have indicated to him that Japanese air strength in the Philippines was severely diminished.

What stood out was the scarcity of flyable Japanese aircraft. Between our fighter sweeps, Kamikaze attrition and the big bomber runs around Christmas there were only maybe 20-30 combat ready Japanese aircraft left in the PI. Where they were and how much fight was left in them remained to be seen.

To put it quite simply, intelligence indicated he was running out of war. Tommie had already done far more than his share in that effort. Indeed, when the Philippines campaign opened he had shot down a Japanese fighter on his initial approach to the new base at Tacloban. For that he received an ovation from the ground crew witnesses after which he famously remarked..."my kinda war zone, I like it where you have to blast your way onto the air strip."

Getting back to the story. On this night, studying the photo and recon intel he would have seen his most likely area to find the enemy would be one of the many airfields on Negros Island.

He had gathered up some solid guys to go with him including his old friend from Alaska flying days Major Rittmayer. Shortly after sun up on 7 Jan 45 they were in the air and on the hunt. What had to be going through his mind was three more to become number one. Two to match, three to win. For the last few months it had been a target rich environment, a fighter pilots dream.   The quality of the opposition had steadily diminished since Rabaul collapsed and now the numbers had really thinned. The Japs were always dangerous but, everyone knew they were typically flying against green horns. He had just had a run of 7 down in the 48 hours covering 25-27 Dec. That put him at 38 confirmed kills. With Bong back in the states it was all within reach.

In pursuit of that goal they headed for Fabrica airdrome. In that immediate area and flying at about 1500 feet and just under a thin overcast they soon caught sight of an enemy fighter low to the left front of the flight leader. He was approaching from the front at about 500 foot altitude.

At the sighting Daddie Green flight responded and the command was issued by Major McGuire to turn left in pursuit and specifically to "not drop belly tanks." This was a violation of his own written directive as well as to never engage a Zero in a dogfight at low speed or low altitude. Many, many people have pondered these contradictory decisions over and over. Why he willingly violated his own precepts is any ones opinion. I think it was a combination of things all coming together at the wrong moment in time.

Tom like many others had been flying combat more or less continuously for over two years. Yes, he had been on some short leaves and he had spent about 3 months in '43 recovering from wounds. But, mostly he had been in the thick of it hammering at the enemy day after day. He had been promoted to Commander of the 431ST Squadron at age 23. A lot of responsibility at any age. He was a very good commander and leader. Tommie was a working Commander who flew combat as often as he could. Tommie was a high wire guy, he had energy way beyond normal. I think the stress of it all affected his judgment, that and his quest to beat Bong. He was very much aware the Japanese were folding and the targets were few in the PI. zone.

They never sent him back to the states, think about it. He was one of the very few who did not get rested stateside. I blame Gen Kenney for that but, then, I don't. Kenney loved all of those kids. He was a middle aged ex WWI fighter pilot and he understood their passion so, he let them stay on in pursuit of their ambition.

Above all of that McGuire really lusted to be "Ace of Aces". For Bong it was a job to do and it led him to that place. For Tom it was a burning quest for first place. He was very competitive his whole life. In addition he would likely soon be promoted to Lt Col and it was for certain he would be awarded a Congressional Medal of Honor in the near future. He made no secret of wanting to go career after the war ended. Sew this title up and he had nothing but green lites and a great career ahead of him. His ambition was likely overriding his sense of caution. Tommie made that turn in pursuit of destiny, and it all started working against him.

He was reaching for the brass ring and he was making mistakes. It was very unlike him but, he made them in multiples and it cost him his life. It is said that he turned too tight...too slow...too low, and with the burden of the drop tanks that he stalled and rolled in.

No one to this day has an answer to how these events unfolded. It is all speculative and I'll not try to unravel it. Witnesses survived on both sides. What is known is that minutes later Tommie and Major Rittmayer were both burning on the jungle floor. One of the Japanese was also hit and wounded. He struggled back to his base where he pancaked short and was shot dead in the cockpit by Filipino guerillas watching from the jungle. The rest went home and survived the war. How bizarre does it get?

Jack Ball Rittmayer in a Naval Academy dress uniform, he later switched to the US Army Air Force where he saw combat, 1942.

Somehow with the loss of Tom McGuire the 431ST was never the same again. The 475TH GRP chugged on but, they seemed to deflate and just kind of drifted along until the end of the war. It was Johnson and the 49TH

Charles Lindeburg (l.) and Tom McGuire. Lindeburg used his transatlantic flight experience to teach the pilots how to extend the range of the P-38s.

that kept steaming along and they got the honor of escorting MacArthur into Atsugi naval Air Station when we took over Japan.

That's the story on Tom McGuire son, as much as is known. Even 50 years later it is hard to understand how this happened. So much of it just doesn't make sense. Tommie was the best at flying the P-38 of anyone I ever saw fly one. He wore that airplane like a skin. It became almost like a living animal in his hands. For him to lose the feel of that airplane and thus crash it is just hard to grasp. One of his co-flyers who flew wing to him many, many times summed it up I think the best. He said that "in his zeal to be number one he had just...reached too far."

Right about the time the story ended the bottom began to

fall out of the darkened sky. When that began the old pilot hustled off to the dry comfort of the Buick and headed homeward. I pedaled homeward in a down pore, my only solace, that it was a warm August rain as can only occur in Wisconsin.

Starting later that night I began to research Tom McGuire and this whole incident. The old pilot was right. There is much speculation, and very little fact. The end result just leaves a lot of open enededness. What it did lead to was discovering the greatness of our second place fighter Ace. There is a lot out there about this man and I've tried to visit all I can find. He had to have been as good as everyone says, maybe even better than many understood.

In everything I've read he is still the only man I've ever read about who flew so well and so far beyond design that he could bend his airplane and not tear it apart. That was Tommie McGuire Jan 1945.

Three on a Match... The Death Of A Legend

In the time and space between his arrival New Years Eve 1945 at San Francisco and the night of 5 August 45 Richard and Marge Bong shared a life of adulation, celebrity and newly wed bliss. At that time Major Bong was known to probably everyone in America. The Government used him to sell bonds to fund the war and for public relations to keep the whole national effort on track to its conclusion. It was clear to all by early 1945 that we would force surrender, it was just a matter of when. Richard had ascended to the level of a National Treasure. He would not see combat again in this war.

He had achieved a mantel of privilege and used it to enter into training in the revolutionary new P-80 jet fighter just coming on stream. This was the future of military aviation and Richard was staged to ride the cutting edge. Accordingly he was sent to the Army Air Forces development base, Wright Patterson Field in Ohio for flight and class room training in all aspects of this new technology. After a few months of this he was assigned to test pilot development work at the Lockheed facilities at Burbank, California.

This suited both him and his new wife well. They both liked the warm, sunny California life style which included for them interaction socially with important people and famous Hollywood personalities of the day. This was a good milieu for Richard at this time in his life. He reportedly was not yet sure whether to continue a career in the military or to cross over to civilian life. For certain he intended to stay in aviation even if he got out of the Army. In this new assignment it was a given he could have become a civilian test pilot if he chose to.

In the summer of 1945 he entered into a pleasant routine of test flying, socializing, golf, and domestic comfort. They were young, he 24 and she 22 and full of energy and promise. There was for Richard and Marge a constant whirl of parties to attend. On the night of 5 August 45 he and Marge attended one of these friend hosted events. It was not to be a late night affair Richard had a mid-day test hop scheduled for the morrow. There was light drinking of course and everyone smoked, it was 1945, everyone did, including Dick and Marge. It was trendy, almost like an accessory. Being young they shared in the cool cache of youthful knowing along with others.

In the days that followed many in attendance would recall that just hours before his demise Richard would openly test an old, old soldiers taboo. Specifically, on the third occasion that evening as he was seen to be the third person to light his cigarette off the same match someone broached that taboo. When lit he is quoted to have replied..."Let me blow the match out and thereby remove the curse". Whereby he did, blow it out, everyone laughed and the night moved on. Twelve hours later Americas greatest fighter pilot was gone.

Let us now discuss that final flight the following day. At about 2:30 P.M. on the afternoon of 6 August 1945 Richard Bong lifted his experimental P-80 Shooting Star jet fighter into a clear blue California sky and less than 30 seconds later America's Ace of Aces was dead. Somewhere between lift off and the end of the runway the revolutionary bird began to fail him. Richard Ira Bong true to his character and knowing he was losing flight integrity guided his stricken craft away from nearby homes. Skillfully he threaded his way between power lines to an empty patch of ground nearby and crashed. Many people witnessed this event and it was clear to all he selflessly drove his aircraft to a safe crash sight to avoid harming innocent bystanders and residents. He tried to save himself too. He was seen to leap from the sinking aircraft but, too late and too low for his parachute to deploy properly. Mercifully he perished on contact with the ground his parachute strung out but not opened lying behind his motionless body. After two years of intense air combat and 40 confirmed kills a superior warrior whom the enemy never touched or shot down lay dead in a field in Burbank, California. Just nine days before victory in the Pacific. Taken by the emerging technology of the future, just as one door was opening another closed. Richard was still, his broken body straddling the pathway at age 24. A shocked America woke to the news and it is a testament to his popularity that even the nuclear bombing of Japan did not overshadow his passing as the reportage of his death received equal front page billing in major news print throughout the land. Within days Major Bong was buried with full military honors in a serene setting in his hometown of Poplar, Wisconsin. In his honor 18 P-47 fighters circled his graveside ceremony in one final salute.

The End Is Near Pilot Monologue:

Reassessing *As The End Nears*, I found this late war analysis in a three page letter form next to his first similar diary entry. It looks like he had intended to send it to someone and never got around to it. Although it is similar it does share even more conviction. By the time of writing this instrument he had seen the massive destruction of our resources. In addition it shows he was already planning for post war events.

The Pilot Monologue

The first half of the war in the Pacific started with the expansion to create the perimeter defense and to secure vital raw materials for the war effort in China the Pacific War and the home industrial base. That effort was intended to include the conquest of Australia. The initial halt took place at the Battle of the Coral Sea. Our ambition had led us to this moment as we prepared to subjugate Australia. Our land forces were in charge of New Guinea and our Navy was on it's way to take Port Moresby as the stage area to attack Australia. The Americans fought us to a draw in the first carrier battle in history in April of '42. The disaster at Midway in June had been carefully hidden away. In the first half of the year we had strengthened our hand but, by August the Americans had come ashore at Guadalcanal and seized our newly constructed air field. It was like a dagger in a jugular.

Starting then the battle raged ever and ever more intense. We lost our foot hold at Henderson Field but, we stood them up still in New Guinea. That battle was for the most part fought in the air. It was more like a siege. It was 3 dimensional and it surged back and forth over some of the wildest and most inhospitable terrain on earth. Strategic posts and strong points mostly supported bomber and fighter bases. Near the equator the weather was ferocious. It was constantly hot and sticky with violent storms frequent and covering much of the land mass as well as surrounding waters.

It was difficult to move on the terrain as roads basically

did not exist. This was wild, verdant jungle. Supplies had to come by air and they were always sparse with food at times scarce. Still, we fought them tenaciously. Slowly they inched us back suffering high casualties in fierce ground fighting as well as significant losses in the air. By the summer of '44 they had pretty well pushed us out of New Guinea. We hung on a while in the Solomons but, by January February of '44 we were finished at Rabaul and it all began to focus on the Philippines. By October of 1944 the second phase Battle of the Pacific was in full swing. We were now clearly on the defensive. The days of giddy expansion had become a receding memory. Instead of conquest we now fought to retain what was left with the over arching imperative of keeping the enemy out of the homeland. Ultimately, to somehow pressure them to a peaceful settlement that would retain the historic polity intact.

By the fall of 1944 the U.S had established a foothold on the East Coast of Leyte. The Army Air Force had two big fighter bases at Tacloban and Dulag. The US Navy had 3,000 ships in and around the waters to support it's forays against our forces. Much of this was a supply train of transport ships stretching a boat every 23 minutes from the PI. to the ports on the West coast. Carrier task forces darted in and out on three day attack sprints like wolves after prey. The great Yamamoto was correct...we had awoken the giant and he flailed us mercilessly. As for us. We had several hundred airstrips and 3,000 combat aircraft in place when the center of gravity shifted to the Philippines. At the highest levels it was clear we were literally being overwhelmed with industrial output and determined, dedicated manpower. Out of desperation, in this painful milieu our leaders turned to a suicide attack policy. It was a drastic step yes, but, in the end turned out to be the most effective weapon system we employed during the course of the war. I myself as well as other experienced pilots were spared as we were needed to shepherd neophytes to the targets. Ultimately our skills would be needed to defend the skies of the homeland as the war rolled to our shores.

It was brave youth that paid the price while our hearts pained for their loss. War is a terrible game...as players men do what they must do even when you are losing.

So there we were slugging it out day after day until by January February '45 the PI. Theater was devoid of operable Japanese aircraft. About 1500 Navy and about 500 Army aircraft had been lost in Kamikaze attacks alone. This is how many were flown from the mainland as replacements. The rest about 3,000 aircraft were pre-staged at over 200 bases in the Philippines The rest were combat attrition, mostly fighters in support of defense and attacks by Kamikaze. As our presence wore down we shifted our seasoned survivors to Iwo-Jima me included, Formosa and most to the homeland. After all of our aircraft at Iwo were destroyed the last remaining pilots about 25 men myself included were transferred to units in the home islands.

I spent the early spring of '45 shepherding Kamikaze flights from strike bases on Kyushu to target points off Okinawa. Steadily we succumbed until Okinawa fell and we were redirected to homeland aerial defense. I spent my last days of the war dicing with U.S Navy fighter sweeps and B-29 bomber formations both intent on our destruction. I flew combat right up through the last hours before the Emperors speech. Like everyone else I was both stunned to hear his voice and shocked at the abrupt change in reality. Like it or not we obeyed...by the millions.

As I mulled the new reality the validity of a plan suddenly occurred to me and without further contemplation I proceeded to effect it. I would have one more flight in my fighter. Not for my Emperor, not for the Navy, not for my countrymen or fellow aviators but, for myself. One last flight of fancy...the pathway to a new unknown.

Coming Home: The Last Flash Of The Sword

Through the night of 14-15 August Capt Bano slept little. His mind racing, he kept hearing the Emperors proclamation on the 14TH that Japan had surrendered, the war was over. Interspersed with that he kept revisiting memories of the war. Combat actions, beer drinking with fellow flyers, his combat victories, his injury and recovery, the brief visits with his new wife.

Like many others he had known for some time, it was inevitable Japan would lose. Still, when the time came it was a shock . By dawns light he had made his decision. He would confiscate one of the fighters and fly home to his family. Very carefully he packed his white dress uniform and personal keepsakes. Not much but mementoes dear to him along with his Navy personnel records.

Last he grabbed his families 350 year old Samurai sword stepped out of the barracks and hailed a passing vehicle and directed the driver to take him to the aircraft revetments area. When they arrived he directed the driver towards a shiny new AM6 Zero. If the driver suspected anything out of order he kept it to himself. After all this man was a well respected fighter pilot.

Like everyone else the driver knew the war was over. Whatever the Capt was up to was his business. Thus he left the area vowing to himself he knew nothing of the captain's presence on the ramp.

Meanwhile Capt Bano loaded his personal items into the luggage compartment and began a quick pre-flight walk around concluding with draining the water from the fuel tanks as a safety measure. He was very pleased with this airplane. It was brand new having been produced in the underground production facility just a few days before and flown into the base yesterday. The war was still on then and it had been fueled and ammunition loaded fresh.

It was combat ready which pleased the Capt and he quickly removed the wheel chocks and various warning flags and loaded them into storage. Assured everything was in order he climbed aboard slid the canopy back and eased himself into the seat. Last he stowed the sword securely next to his seat as he had done every time he flew combat during the war.

As quick as possible he started the engine and without waiting for normal warm up he guided the aircraft along the taxi way and out to the main runway. Once on the runway he looked into the distance in both directions making sure there were no other flights coming in. He did not contact the tower for permission to launch.

Indeed he had made sure his radio was turned off when he climbed aboard. He was sure the control tower was in a frenzy trying to figure out who and what was going on. All military operations had been told to stand down. All aircraft were to be disabled. In addition, all Japanese pilots were forbidden to fly for ten years. With that in mind he gave the Zero full power and was soon clawing his way to two hundred feet where he banked left and headed out toward the sea just a few miles away.

He flew fast and low for about 20 miles, well out of sight of the land he had just left. At that point he banked right and flew about 15 miles maintaining his speed and altitude. There was a natural hook in the land in this area and when he saw it he turned back toward the mainland. This was an area he knew well and as he passed the shore line he was headed due West as planned. He didn't fear pursuit by his own forces but, he was keenly aware that should he encounter US fighters they likely would shoot him down.

Within minutes he came upon a small inland village and when he passed it he cut his speed back to a leisurely 180 MPH slid the canopy back and let the moist August air swirl freshly in the cockpit. From here on he followed a meandering stream through valleys and small mountains. It was a beautiful cloudless day and he kept low so he could see the peasants at work in the fields and smell the freshness of the earth and pine forests.

This was territory he knew from childhood on and he began to feel better about this whole idea. This was a serious offense. Not only would the Americans be outraged if they found out about this but, even more consequential he had stolen the Emperor's property. If caught that might even warrant capitol punishment. Knowing all this he flew on with a smile on his face. If he could just reach the big valley just past the up coming mountain range he would be safe.

As he approached the mountains he raised his speed to 300MPH and when he crossed the peaks he saw the wide verdant expanse before him. Here there were grain fields and orchards many different crops as well as large stands of bamboo cultivated for aesthetics. Along the trails here and there were farm hands tending to this and that. To the North against a natural cliff stood the Lord of The Manors columned castle. It was elevated about 100 feet so the master could observe all of his domain at his leisure. There were paved areas as well with the main road leading from the courtyard of the castle to the far side of the valley where stood a small mountain covered with vegetation and pines. The entire estate covered hundreds of acres and had been in the Lords family for generations. This was a very powerful and influential man. Indeed his power was such that he was immune to interference from

Tokyo. Bano knew all this and knew that he was now safe from prosecution for his bold actions.

Capt Bano soaked all this in and when satisfied he drove his Zero to 5,000 feet and at 2/3 power began an aerial demonstration few had ever seen. He did inside loops, and outside loops. He snap rolled, he did wing overs, chandelles, a clover leaf and flew a full circle inverted just for good measure. As a finale he took a high speed low pass up the paved road towards the Manor pulling up into a loop at the last moment and positioned for a landing he gently set the Zero down on the road and coasted to a stop just short of the mountain on the far side.

As he crawled out of the cockpit an ornate and gilded hand carrier pulled up next to the airplane and out stepped the Lord of The Manor himself. Hitting the ground Capt Bano bowed deeply and quietly awaited acknowledgement from the Lord. Motioning the Capt to stand straight the Lord turned to his assistant and directed him to gather all hands and to remove the mountain camouflage, open the steel doors and roll the airplane into the inner garage area. That done he turned his attention back to Capt Bano. "Tell me what you've been up to Bano." "Yes sir. I took it upon myself to come home in the Emperors fighter sir as a gift to you. We have lost the war but, we did our best against horrendous odds. I thought you might like to add the Zero to the Hall of Warriors. My families Samurai sword is in the cockpit so it can be returned to display. It served me well for inspiration and I'm sure protection from harm. It accompanied me on every combat mission."

With that Bano took the Lord on a tour of the aircraft pointing out various features and performance capabilities as well as an outline of the war success of the fighter. As he finished the tour the ground crews showed up and rolled the aircraft toward the garage opening. In a matter of minutes it was safe inside and the crews set to work returning the camouflage items to the mountain side.

Turning to Bano the Lord explained that a glass case would be built to protect the aircraft from deterioration. He also planned a likeness of the Capt in his full flight uniform to stand next to the aircraft. A second display would have him in his dress Naval uniform for display in the Hall of Warriors.

Capt Bano was beside himself. In the 400 year history of the Hall there had never been two honorariums to one Warrior. The Lord was very pleased with his contribution in the war effort and the presentation of this prized possession.

Like all the other Warrior contributors the Bano family had worked these lands for generations. It was a symbiotic relationship where the workers received one third of their production, adequate housing and assistance such as medical care when needed. For them their situation was ideal. Their loyalty unquestioned, over time when the nation needed help the young men often volunteered for service to the country.

The Lord was very proud of his extended family as well as his predecessors who long ago established the shrine within the mountain. Now, Capt Bano would occupy a special niche in that heritage for all time.

As he finished his pledge to the displays the Lord turned to Bano and asked. "Is there anything I can do for you now young man?"

"Yes sir could you please provide a couple of horses so I can make it to my home before sundown". "It is just over the mountains to the East and I would like to get there today. I have not seen my wife in eighteen months".

"Very well young man your desire is granted. I was hoping to have you stay with me for lunch but, this is far more important and we can dine together another time". With that he ordered one of his men to return quickly with two horses and to accompany the Capt to his home. He then entered the transporter and returned to his Manor.

The horseman soon arrived and they began their ascent

in an area naturally lower than the surrounds. There were no roads in this section but, a light trail had been worn in by the daily passage of workers to and from the estate. Because of the up and down it took about an hour on foot. Astride the horses they made the crossing in about a half hour.

Once over and on the flat land it was just a few minutes until Bano stood at the gate to his small farm. He sent the horseman on his way opened the gate and headed for the traditional thatched roof house. Everything was clean and tidy and he could see the stone pathway leading to the door had been swept. As he took this in his wife opened the door and ran the last 20 feet to greet him.

As they embraced she began to weep. Overcome with emotion she dropped to her knees and continued hugging him. "Oh Bano I am so happy, it is over and you are home safe".

"Yes my dear I am safe and home to stay".

He then pulled her to her feet and hugged her for a long time gently rocking from side to side as he did so. Finally he leaned back and said "Let's go inside and talk. Let me tell you how I got here and the many things I've done in the last few years. Japan lost the war, but, we survived it. How lucky we are, we still have each other and the future belongs to us."

This is my reconstruction of the day my Uncle came home from the war. It is taken from the entries in his diary. Together he and his wife started anew. It could be said, like a fairy tale "they lived happily ever after" and they did.

As for me this is where my story ends with one final anecdote. Upon finishing my masters degree I was contacted by an emissary of the estate and invited to a visit there. Transport arrangements were made and I was instructed to dress formally for an evening dinner to honor my Uncle and myself.

I was given a tour of the Hall of Warriors by the Lord himself including being allowed to enter the cockpit of my Uncles fighter. What a grand experience. I was thrilled as I grasped the control stick and worked my feet on the control pedals. Below me to the right was the likeness of my Uncle in his flight gear replete with the 350 year old Samurai sword at his waist. It really hit me then. These were exceptional people who manned these machines, their sacrifices should never be forgotten.

The dinner was grand and went on for hours. I was allowed to sit next to the Lord, we talked about many things and he seemed pleased with my presence. When it was over he invited me to return anytime I felt the need to commiserate with my Uncle.

This is where my story ends. Inspired by the diary and the heritage of the Hall of Warriors I felt an obligation to illuminate and share these insights from my Uncles experience.

In Conclusion

As it is in all things, this story too has an end, thus it follows. In time I came to understand that Uncle had entrusted me, his young niece, to tell his story. He was a very brave man, a very good man. He and his co-flyers were for the most part...all good men. They served faithfully and performed magnificently in the evil game of war. They were ordinary simple people whose other wise uneventful existence would have gone unnoticed. In the end they were all victims of evil men. Manipulators of power who made foolish decisions resulting in the destruction of lives and wealth. Men who bandied about with three year old egos and thoughtless ambition. Men who were all old enough to know better had betrayed the polity to the point of stone age ruin.

Early in the war they were cheered as they marched into the lands of their Asian brothers. After all, they were freeing them from the yoke of Colonialism. Soon the cheering stopped as the arrogance and cruelty of the new masters stripped away the naiveté of the hosts. As for Uncle and his surviving comrades, they waded through the calamity as best they could. Eventually the allies prevailed, the maiming and the dying ended, and slowly, they came home to pick up the pieces.

Uncle, though badly wounded during the war, had recovered by wars end, and with his wonderful and patient wife went on to eventual prosperity. She preceded him in death by ten years. As a man who endured much death of close comrades in war he took her passing stoically. They had children but, no girls and I think he saw me as a substitute daughter. He spent much time with me from little on and it is fair to say I adored him like a second father. That is why he entrusted me with his diary and his story. I am so very grateful for the privilege. To me he was a great man although but a small piece in that huge and tragic struggle. Though the cause was unjust I am proud of him for his loyalty to sovereign and service to his countrymen.

It was late now on the day, the sun still above the Roko Mountains but, sinking. As I rose from the bench to depart the wind stirred and a cascade of cherry petals fell about me. One in particular lightly brushed my cheek and lighted upon the flat and closed diary. Noticing this I sat back down, grasped the blossom gently and slid it beneath the now partially opened cover. I squeezed it shut to maintain the shape, rose and headed for home.

This then concludes the story of my Uncle, Imperial Japanese Navy fighter pilot in the great Pacific War. I hope you enjoyed it.

Col Johnson: The General Custer of WWII

It was mid morning when I arrived at the fishing spot and sure enough the old pilot was already at work teasing the currents. He was playing a surface popper near the undercut on the far bank. Seeing this I thought to myself, crappie and blue gill beware you could be headed for suppers frying pan. I said "hello" and he welcomed me as I seated myself on the nearby log.

It was one of those cool, crisp, clear sky mornings that only occur in "God's Country" as the locals refer to the area. It had been still on my arrival but, shortly thereafter, a breeze had suddenly kicked up. You could actually hear it coming from the Northwest. First it whispered the tall pines, then it raced across the meadow bending the low growth before it. As it reached the willows edging the stream it snapped the lower branches hard enough to lift the slender leaves from the water momentarily. As the graceful willow heaved and danced I could suddenly see the ripples on the water as the first blast passed.

It then became a strong, steady wind that did not yield. It was a sign of approaching winter. This far North the arctic tongue would reach down and lick even in mid August. If you stayed in the sun it was very pleasant, if you entered shadow it would soon chill. We stayed in the sun. It was rich and warm this time of year. As the earth begins to tilt and the rays stretch through more air the color of the sunlight changes to

119

a golden yellow. It is almost as though it glows and it is so intense it deepens shadows. It is such a pleasant experience the memory of scenes becomes indelible. This then was such a moment.

The old man was enjoying it too. The fish were not biting and pretty soon he laid his rod aside, then turned to face me with his elbows on his thighs and his hands joined between his slightly spread knees. As he did this he began to speak. "I've talked to you a lot about my fellow pilots and our activities long ago. All that I've spoken of were great people and many were good friends. Actually I've mentioned this guy before but, today I want to talk to you about Col. Johnson at length." His story is as follows.

Gerald R. Johnson was from Eugene, Oregon and he came to the SWPA with McGuire, Watkins and Wally Jordan. They all came down from the Aleutians in late '42. Jerry had gotten two kills in a P-39 while flying out of Kiska. That was no small feat in itself. Initially he flew P-40's out of Moresby. I met him at Dobo after he made the move to the P-38 and he flew with the 49TH...The Flying Knights.

I wasn't in his unit but, I drank with him at the club and I flew missions alongside his unit. I saw him fly and I saw him fight. He was a phenomenon. Anybody who went up with Jerry knew immediately they were flying with a natural. Ralph Wandrey once told me that the first time he flew wing with him he understood that sticking with Jerry meant that he was good enough to survive the war, and he did. Jerry and McGuire and maybe Neel Kirby were probably the best fighter pilots in the Pacific.

Along with that he was a great leader. A man who feared nothing and took it to the enemy like he was invincible. Early on he was nicknamed "Johnnie Eager" because he volunteered to fly beyond the duty schedule. By the time he was 21 he was a squadron commander. By the time he was 23 he had been sent to the Command and General Staff

College at Fort Leavenworth Kansas. When he came back to the theater in the fall of '44 he was a Lt Col. and was placed as Deputy Commander of the 49TH. By the spring of '45 he was promoted to full Colonel and at the age of 24 assumed command of the 49TH Fighter Group. This is almost unheard of.

In spite of all his responsibilities he still managed to shoot down 24 enemy aircraft. The guy loved a fight and he loved to fly. On his off time he learned to fly the twin engine bombers. He especially loved the B-25 Mitchell and he would roll them over airdromes for grins. He even shot down an Australian fighter, an accident of course. Fortunately the pilot was not injured. He painted the Aussie flag on his nose along with the Jap kills. A month later he was himself machine gunned by a trigger happy B-25 waist gunner. This happened right over Gusap. He was not personally injured and immediately crash landed his stricken craft, and laughed about it.

One time on Leyte he led a flight of 12 P-38s against a Jap convoy and it is estimated they destroyed around 200 vehicles and killed 3500 Japanese troops thus thwarting a planned counter attack. I should emphasize here. To lead a low level ground attack against such numbers was extremely dangerous. Many might have even considered it fool hardy. Not Jerry, he viewed it as an opportunity and his duty. On a famous combat flight off Leyte he shot down three enemy aircraft in 45 seconds. They showed the gun camera footage in fighter school for years afterward.

Probably one of his most flamboyant moments was the wing attack on the Jap emplacements along the Ipo Dam stronghold. This was a first of a kind attack. He led his men in flights of 16 abreast while dropping napalm canisters en masse. He led this just like a Cavalry charge, right out in front, wave after wave through the pitching conflagration. It turned the Japanese defenses to ash and that was the end of resistance at Ipo.

He survived the war but, died in a typhoon over Tokyo Bay in October of '45. Beyond his flying skill he was the kind of leader men would follow into the fires of hell without a second thought. Men did, and considered it a privilege. That was Johnnie Eager...The General Custer of WWII.

Suddenly it was all over for the day. The fish refused to bite but, the wind did. When the story ended so did the days activities. The ex pilot packed his gear, said "goodbye" and aimed his Buick for home. As he drove away he commented that with an empty creel he thought he might treat his wife to a steak dinner down town. We both laughed, I mounted my bike and pedaled for home my thoughts busy trying to image the events he had just described.

It wasn't until much later in the evening, after I had bedded down. As I lay staring into the dark it finally hit me. This Johnnie Eager guy was something else. Everything he did was bigger than life. Fighter pilot at 21. Squadron Commander at 22. That's 16 aircraft and men to lead into battle. Group Commander rank of full Colonel at age 24. That's 48 fighters and about 700 personnel to manage and lead into battle. Just one step from becoming a General officer. Commander of the highest scoring fighter group in the Pacific. 24 combat victories of his own. An Ace four times over. An innovator of fighter bomber ground attack tactics blending an old world cavalry charge with modern technologies of aircraft and napalm. As I mulled all this the question kept coming to mind. How could a guy that young do all of that?

Between the telling of the story and the charm of the day I was once again in ...a perfect place. With the recap of events and the wonderment of it swirling in my head I drifted into slumber.

The Aftermath: Two Wives, Two Different Men, Two Sad Stories

One day in late August we met at the cemetery just after lunch. He had asked me to meet him there the day before. I arrived a few minutes ahead of schedule and as I waited for him astride my bike in the parking lot I gazed about the grounds. It was an idyllic, tranquil setting. The sky was bright blue and clear the temperature ideal probably about 70 degrees. It's a big cemetery for such a small town and it is basically surrounded by tall pines and also a lot of mature fir trees. There are not so many large trees in the burial parts but, there are a few and indeed there is one large deciduous type adjacent to the area where the Bongs lie.

The grounds were as always well manicured and the grass was rich and green. A gentle breeze stirred now and then with a pleasant whisper in the graceful pines. It is a different kind of resting place for a national hero. There are no statues of men on horses, no marble mausoleums to house the remains. No pomp, no excess, only simple descriptive stones and a beautiful and pleasant landscape.

When the old pilot arrived we greeted each other and began a slow walk over to the area of Major Bongs grave. Initially we chatted lightly about little of substance and when we reached the grave site he bowed his head and we observed a moment of silence. After a bit the old man began to speak and this is how it went. "As you might have guessed I brought you here for a reason." He first asked me if I knew anything about Marge Bong. I replied only that I was aware of her having been married to Major Bong for a while before his death. "Well"...he said. In that case we shall spend some time speaking of her and Tommie McGuire's wife Marilyn as well. To start you've no doubt noticed that the Marge grave is fairly recent. As I nodded affirmation he continued with "We shall get to that in a bit but, first let us speak of Bong and McGuire comparatively." With that he began the narrative that follows.

So, this is what it came down to, almost to the waning hours of the war. Neither of our greatest Aces survived. In a way their deaths were a paradigm in life somewhat echoing the weapon paradigms they flew. Tom McGuire flying to the aid of a fellow pilot under attack. Richard Bong selflessly guided his falling aircraft away from homes and lives to a deserted patch of land. These were men of substance, they were both strong in personality, responsible and professional. They were men of character and admirable moral fiber. The one was short and stocky the other tall and thin. One was quiet, a man of few words who did not take to excess or braggadocio. The other though surely not a braggart would talk in detail of his air adventures. One was openly ambitious the other almost humble. They were in many ways polar opposites. They were both very good at what they were asked to do. In addition they complemented one another by flying missions together and they were friends. In the end it was a sad loss of them both to family, friends and a sorrowful nation.

Both left young widows. Back in Texas a young Marilyn "pudgy" McGuire got the bad news. Her very special man had perished in combat. It was a common story in those days. A much too short, whirl wind romance. Some, never enough, time together, and then the war called. In Tom's case there never was a "coming home". Though often promised by higher ups, somehow, for Tommie, it never happened.

Years went by and there were only letters and news reports. The widow to be waited patiently and in the end was left with 1942 memories of a man gone. Like thousands of others she would press on with her life, her recall of Tommie forever frozen at age 22. The only consolation was to always have the memories, the pride, and the association with one of our nations greatest heroes.

In this she was not alone. Just a few months later Marge Bong would suffer the same emptiness. A moment of tragedy and it was all gone. Again, the last memories of a man whose image was forever frozen at age 24 would have to last a life time.

In a way the differences in the widows lives had paralleled those of their husbands. They were strange bookends indeed. One quickly became almost as famous as her husband while the other coasted through near obscurity in a cloistered mid Texas town. Marge along with her husband had become nationally known while Marilyn was not even that well known in her home town of San Antonio. The McGuire's had a wedding known only to friends and relatives. The Bongs had a huge Cinderella wedding celebrated by and known to the entire country. Because of his two stateside rest periods and bond drive tours the Bongs were a household name by early 1944. When the final moments came Marge was living a life of celebrity in California while Marilyn worked and waited almost anonymously for her man to return.

Mutually ones grief could not have been any less than the other. Separately they set their wings to the future. In time they both remarried and led normal peace time lives. We had won the war but, for these women and thousands more the scars would last a life time. Fifty eight years later Marge would be laid to rest next to Richard in his hometown of Poplar. It had been a long divided journey but, they were now together again, this time for eternity.

So now you know a little bit more about these two women, wives of our greatest fighter pilots. I wanted to touch on this as they are a part of the story too. I'm sure they were happy for the time they shared but, there lives were forever shadowed by their loss. It is sad and unfortunate but, sometimes in life son the winners lose. I think it important that you know this and it is important that you remember them. Not too long from now I will be joining them it will then be up to folks like yourself to remember them. I've spent quite a bit of time with you this summer covering this story. I think I picked the right guy to carry the ball. I know you won't let me down.

There followed another moment of bowed silence and then it was time for us to leave. But, before we left he thanked me for joining him at this special place. He said it meant a lot to him personally. We left then, he in his Buick and I on my bicycle each headed for home. As I rode along I thought about what he had told me. I thought about Marilyn and I thought about Marge. I thought about how these young men not much older than myself had flashed across history like meteors and how the women in their lives were left to pick up the pieces. These were strong people of great character. Could we ever be as good as they were? I think we can be, only time will tell. What I do know is they have shown us the path. It is up to us now to carry the ball.

Now and Then

By the end of June I had a much better understanding of the story the old man was telling. The old man had arrived in New Guinea almost at the beginning of hostilities. He was not only telling me about these many experiences, he was telling the story in chronological order. As I came to understand this my interest grew ever deeper and I began to spread myself out as I searched for more and more information.

First, I gathered some books on geography making sure they contained adequate maps of the seas and land masses of the South Pacific. After several hours of study I had a much better appreciation of how this great contest unfolded. Once I could define the different land masses from memory I began measuring the distance between important locations. It was soon clear this was a very large battlefield. At its zenith the Empire of Japan covered 20 million square miles. Probably 70 percent of that area was open water. For the US it was as much about transport and supply as it was about ambition. For Japan faced with the same problems it was all multiplied with the need to access raw materials and the necessity to shield its activities.

I spent another night looking at the weather, mountains and jungle. With the proximity to the equator storms were frequent and usually violent. The old man talked about it a lot. He stressed that besides discomfort the weather deviled and vexed their operations often. Sometimes it would save them from the enemy but, even that refuge could be very risky. Mountains reached to 10,000 and 13,000 feet. Passage through them was limited to choke points ideal for aerial ambush and scary to traverse for damaged aircraft or when shrouded in thick clouds. The jungle below was vast, hostile and unforgiving to anyone unfortunate enough to parachute or crash land into its grip. Typically the jungle just swallowed anyone who went into it.

Next I began to look at the military strategy and history of the event. It was complex to say the least yet, fascinating and logical. By the middle of July I had a pretty good background developed and I was getting a lot more out of the old mans stories. Islands, big and small became focal points of contest. Occupation of specific islands provided rings of influence limited only by the range of tactical aircraft. In theory at least overlapping ranges formed a shield over the inner domain ultimately protecting the Japanese home islands and sea lanes. The task of the United States military was to dislodge the Japanese one by one from these bases. This is the story the old man lived starting at the toe hold at Port Moresby, New Guinea in late 1942 and ending in the Philippines in the late fall of 1945. By mid August with the story of the struggle centered on the Philippines I was in step with the Japanese sense of desperation. Conversely the old mans tales spoke of confidence. The aggression was now evident in the hunt and the quest for glory and fame began to burn. The overlay of course was the human factor. The many remembrances from the old mans participation.

By the coming of September the story telling had ended. I was soon on my way back to the city and school. The old flier and his wife would stay for the autumn panorama and then flee to a more hospitable climate. Life moved on, each traveled their separate paths. I never saw the old man again. However, as time went on my interest thus awakened never waned. I thought about him often.

It occurred to me on an occasion, it was an interesting paradox. Through the spring and summer the old man conversationally had relived his youth. Now in the autumn of his life he reached back through time and with clarity and the judgement of maturity imparted to me all that he knew. I as the young man became the vicarious participant in battles of old. I owe much to that experience. It awoke my interest, widened my perception and ultimately caused me to become more scholarly and purposeful.

From that summer on everything took on a new importance. Some of that was for sure reaching the age of 16 but, most of the maturing was caused by this happy communion. Even my mother noticed the difference on my return. I had noticed early on when the old flyer started talking about the war. He would talk about individuals by name or he would describe in detail what happened on a given day but, he seldom talked about where they came from or how they looked or talked, etc. It occurred to me that he saw them as they were in their youth. He was reliving these scenes as if it were yesterday. It was as if I was there next to him thus there was no need of detailed description. It worked for him and I guess in the end it worked for me.

The Ledger

Original Bong Memorial in Poplar, WI

I rode my bike down Main St. Made a left onto Brent Dr, rode the two blocks further and there to my left and across the street tucked into the South end of the brick grade school stood the Richard Bong Memorial Center. Opened in 1955 and shoe horned into the building of a new grade school and financed by the county and a public bond. A likeness of the P-38 Dick flew in combat made an attractive addition on a pylon next to the building. I then walked the twenty feet to the entrance opened the left side of the double door and stepped into the foyer. If you were to turn left here you would enter the gymnasium. I turned right, passed through the open door frame six feet away and stepped back in time.

It is a small room about 20 by 14 feet made of simple concrete block with glass on the South and West walls and a low tiled ceiling. Two 50's airline terminal loungers, a similar one person seat, a small metal desk and chair in one corner to sit and reflect. Next to the desk a 2 ½ foot tall 3 inch metal pipe with a cap and a slot in the top for those inclined to donate to property maintenance.

Photos, articles, and mementoes adorn the walls and fill the single glass encasement. In the Southwest corner stands

a life size bronze statue of Maj. Bong. Opposite on the East
end a wall to wall glassed case with all of his medals and surviving artifacts including his combat parachute, parts of the
P-80 that took his life and the 48 star US flag still neatly tri-
folded from his funeral. On the back wall of the glass case are
posted the certificates of his 35 combat and campaign awards.
His dress uniform adorned with the Medal Of Honor is centered among the many items on display.

All around the room are pictures of Richard and his co-
flyers. Mostly they are from the 49TH Fighter Group however,
some are from the early days at Port Moresby with the 39TH
Fighter SQ. Still others are with members of the 431ST Fighter
SQ Satan's Angels crowd whom he flew with often throughout
his combat career. Indeed his last four kills in December of
1944 were all achieved while flying with his old buddies in the
431ST.

On the North wall adjacent to the door stands a small dais
with a visitor sign in log. Nothing fancy here it is a simple 3
ring binder with lined note paper. The pages are neatly pre
sectioned with vertical separators and short headers for: date,
origin of visitor, name of visitor and a space for remarks on
the far right.

I had come here on this cold, damp chilly day in early September to study this ledger. I had it in mind for a long time to
do this and as I entered the warm, dry room and removed my
jacket I sensed somehow I had made the perfect choice on a
day such as this.

If a man achieves greatness in life there is typically a
record of his achievements. Usually historians document
what he did, when and where. Some notables have done
this also in Richards case. However, somehow this never
resurrected his steadily waning story. A national hero known
to almost everyone in America had for sure by the time
of the mid sixties become an unknown. A fair number of
war historians, patriots and aviation enthusiasts have kept

the flame alive but, barely. Those who do are ardent and respectful admirers. Unlike people of great enduring fame Richards legacy is now reflected in the ledger. Follow me now through my discovery.

I walked immediately to the dais removed the ledger and carried it over to the airport lounger where I positioned myself comfortably to the armrest. Next I closed the ledger and then reopened it at the first page and began to carefully study the entries. Actually I initially focused on where the visitors came from. After just a few pages one thing stood out. For the most part they came a long way. Not just from distant places in the US but, from all over the world. Poplar, Wisconsin is located in the far North just West of the Great Lake Superior. It is a long difficult journey to arrive at this place even for Wisconsin residents. Even flying in it is basically out of the way and connecting to the Superior airport would dissuade many from coming. To travel by land is a long, long journey from anywhere. Yet, people do come here to visit this memorial because they want too. As I read further I was stunned by the number of visitors from the British Commonwealth. The Prime Minister of Japan on a rare stateside visit came here to honor this man. Other notable Government officials and famous names dot the record.

Too numerous to list individually let us concentrate on a few entries as well as how far and where they have come from. Rays of interest emanating out from this small room like threads in a web reaching vast distances to the far corners of the earth. One visitor a day on average. I counted them 26 pages 23 lines to a page. Some days 2 to 6 entries, some days none. On average, one logged entry per day. Many of those are a party of 2 or more. Children are often included by name and age. In the comments section everyone gracious and thankful for all that Richard did. Even some of his old flying buddies have signed in. Some of them unit support people, cooks, mechanics, typists what have you. All remember and have gone to great effort and personal expense to arrive here to pay their respects. That is Richards legacy, those who remember keep the flame alive.

The first current ledger entry was dated 21 December 1994. Cindy Watts Cloquet, Minnesota. Visiting on a Wednesday from only 41 miles distance probably in the area for the holidays. That time of year likely bitterly cold, possibly below zero even at noon. Thank you Cindy. Many more US entries followed: Riverside, Lethbridge and Modesto, Ca; Hoquhaiam, WA; Round Rock, TX; Lockport, N.Y.; Memphis, Chandler, and others. 7 July 1998: Jerome [Jerry] Vattendahl, Louisiana. Possibly related to Dicks wife Marge.

Suddenly, very special names jump out. 2 August 1998: Capt. James and Yolanda Bong. Mt. Home AFB, Idaho. Nancy Bong, Milwaukee, WI. 20 November 1996 Masake Morishita: Prime Minister Of Japan. 9 March 1997 Marilena Kostapoulis: London, England Lisa and Ruth Dickerson: Johannesburg, South Africa.."To honor Dick and Our Uncle who flew combat together in the SWPA." I'm sure they were related and made this long hard journey together. Thank you ladies. Choo Chung Chee Taiwan Woo Ha Ti Ha Tokyo 28 August 1996 Kathleen and Bill: Townshend, Australia. From the area of the Amberley Airfield complex. Bruce, Kathy and Bill Rossin: Adelaide Harbor, Australia 18 Aug 2002 Tsuto and Kamiyo Hosono: Japan "We are happy to be here".

And so it went, page after page. Remember this is the latest ledger tally starting in December 1994. There are years and years of them stuck away somewhere with I'm sure a much bigger story to tell.

As I closed the ledger and approached to return it the dais the pandemonium of children set free rolled throughout the building. School was out for the day. As they rushed about and spilled through the doors I could not help but think, what a wonderful place for a Memorial to a national hero. I had been here before and I've always enjoyed the visits. It is probably the only memorial in the US that is in a building and un-attended. There are no docents, curators, administrators, or guides pushing and pulling people. There are no vendors of pins and flags out front, no hot dog and soda stands to detract from tranquility and respect. There are never any lines to await entry. If you did run into a crowd it would likely number no more than 5 or 6 most likely one or two. It was a very special place where you could steep in history undistracted with the feint sounds of children laughing and playing in the background. What a wonderful thing for children to be educated and grow in the shadow of greatness. Some days, if you were lucky, you might even hear them singing. I'm sure Richard would have enjoyed that too. I know I did.

Outside the wind was snapping, it was still damp and chilly. With the daylight fading fast I hopped on my bike and made for home. It was going to be another nasty cold night but, once again I was full of fresh insights and new knowledge to digest. All in all it had been a productive day as far as I was concerned. I could hardly wait to finish supper and hit that computer. As I pedaled up the drive to the back door Adelaide Harbor and Johannesburg kept ringing in my head.

Acknowledgement: Floyd Fulkerson

I first met Floyd around 2004. He was in his mid 80's. He and his wife Brenda were living in quiet retirement on the bank of the Arkansas river in the small town of Scott.

I had been told of this man by a woman friend of his wife. She had read a book about Tom McGuire, *The Last Great Ace* by Charles Martin. Within it Floyd is mentioned several times. She then asked me if I knew who McGuire was and I said yes I knew who Tommie was. She then asked me if I had heard of Floyd Fulkerson and that he had flown with Tommie, Bong and some other notables and I said never.

She then asked, "would you like to meet him? I know his wife well and maybe I can arrange it."

"Of course," I said. "Tomorrow if possible."

"No," she said, "let me talk to Brenda, they are somewhat reclusive and given they don't know you it will require their permission I'll check into it and call you in a few days."

In a few days the call came and I was given Floyd's number. I called him and he invited me to their place the next day. Initially I just wanted to meet him and talk with an experienced WWII fighter pilot. When I got there I had a lot of questions but, admit to feeling a little awkward as I was now in the presence of an accomplished individual who had led an exceptional life. He soon made me feel at ease and we began a long association that lasted until his passing 30 Oct 2017 age 96.

What he told me on that first meeting stunned me with all that he had done in the war and afterward. I guess he liked me from the start because he opened up and talked freely about everything. This was a man who did not talk about his exploits, didn't attend old pilots gatherings etc. He was very humble and did not wear his service on his sleeve.

When it was time to go he told me to call or visit anytime and I did visit the home again but, soon after I moved to Phoenix and afterwards we would talk on the phone. One night after I moved to Phoenix his wife called me and we had a long conversation about their entire life together. Mostly she called to thank me for getting Floyd to tell his story and to tell me in all the years they had been married he had never talked about this to her or friends. As she said I don't know what you did to him but I'm glad you did.

I became so inspired by the whole thing that I did more research and eventually had Floyd's story printed in the Dec 2012 issue of Flight Journal aviation history magazine.

This made everyone very happy. *Wingman To The Aces* was the cover story in that issue and I am grateful and thankful to Flight Journal for having made this happen. With my success in that endeavor I then decided to do a book on Floyd and his fellow fliers in the Pacific War. Although Floyd appears often in the book it is not about him. He is however the inspiration for the book and I used his persona along with several others to mold a composite old pilot story teller.

Thus I wanted to acknowledge Floyd's influence in making this all come to pass. I am grateful and thankful that I had the privilege for more than a decade of knowing this man and the time he so graciously granted me. I also want to thank his wife Brenda for the encouragement she gave to see my way through a book. We had many night time conversations together from which I gained insight into Floyd which in turn helped me to form the story. Thanks ever so much to you both it has been a pleasure knowing you.

Acknowledgement: Dick Rose

Dick Rose, originally from Mayville, Wisconsin, was a late life professional fishing guide in Eagle River, Wisconsin. In the early 60's Dick and I were classmates at Mayville High School.

One day in the fall of 1960 he approached me at lunch break and asked, "John, didn't you live in Superior, Wis for a while?"

"Yes," I replied, "I lived there in the 59-60 school year."

"Did you ever visit the Bong Memorial in Poplar?"

"Yes I did several times while I was in Superior."

"Wow, what a guy," he said. "We were up there on a two week fishing vacation and we stopped in at the memorial one day when it was raining. I had never heard of this guy until then and he's from Wisconsin."

"Yes," I said, "What a shame. I'll guarantee you Dick. You and I are the only two students in this high school who are familiar with him and his achievements."

Obviously Dick was inspired by the visit and he learned a lot more from me and about some other famous pilots as well. We soon graduated and went our separate ways and I did not see him again until the late 70's when I ran into him in a Cadillac dealership in Fond Du Lac, Wis. We visited a bit and he told me he would soon move to Eagle River to become a professional fishing guide. Richard was congenial, charming, smart and very good looking. It wasn't long until he married a local TV news star. This became an important link in the building of the new Bong Memorial in Superior.

Superior is just a hop and a skip from Eagle River and

over time Dick's Interest grew in broadening the exposure of Richard Bong. After a while he had met enough of the right people and together with his wife's expertise they co produced a promotional film to demonstrate and hype a potential new museum in Superior. At some point he arranged a meeting with Marge Vattendahl and some other important people and with the demo tape "sold" his idea.

Collectively they saw the wisdom in making the move and in 1989 Marge set the process in motion by establishing a fund to build the new Bong Memorial. With Marge's blessing both private and commercial business quickly funded the building of a new memorial on the shore of Lake Superior in the town of Superior. It stands there today with easy access by tourists and enclosed against the ferocious Wisconsin winters.

The pylon mounted outdoor P-38 tribute to Dick has been refurbished and stands clean and gleaming in the warmth of the main hall. Along with it are accurate life sized dioramas of war time life in the South Pacific and war making artifacts are readily displayed.

It is an excellent educational site as well as a deserved recognition of Richard Bong. It is now visited by thousands annually rather than a few hundred.

I now wish to thank Richard Rose for generating the enthusiasm, financing and planning of this Memorial. Without his personal efforts this may never have happened. Sadly Dick was taken be a terminal disease in the mid 90's. So, what we have is two unknown school boys in a small town next to nowhere who inspired by greatness each in their own way travelled a destiny over decades to help keep the Richard Bong memory alive. Dick Rose with his memorial and I with my book. I only wish he was still alive to read it.

Recommended Reading

Ace of Aces, The Dick Bong Story, Carl Bong and Mike O'Connor

Aces, William Yenne

Dear Mom So We Have A War, Dick Bong

Dick Bong Ace of Aces, Gen. George C. Kenney

Divine Thunder The Life and Death of the Kamikazes, Bernard Millot

Fire In The Sky The Air War In The South Pacific, Eric M. Bergerud

The Kamikazes Suicide Squadrons Of World War II, Edwin P. Hoyt

The Last Great Ace: The Life Of Major Thomas B. McGuire, Jr., Charles A Martin

Possum, Clover, and Hades, The 475TH Fighter Group In WWII, John Stanaway

Samurai, Saburo Sakai, with Martin Caidin and Fred Saito

Zero, Masatake Okumiya, Jiro Horikoshi, and Martin Caidin

Richard I. Bong Veterans Historical Center:
http://www.bvhcenter.org